SPINDLF~

The L

Francis McCrickard was born ~ ~ has taught
in England, Zambia and Mala ~ extensively in
radio and TV. In 1983 he settle ~ey, West Yorkshire.
The Dead are Listening is his first nov~ and it has been translated
into Danish and Portuguese.

The Dead are Listening

The Dead are Listening

Francis McCrickard

Spindlewood

Published as a Spindlewood paperback in 2001
First published in Great Britain in 1995 by
Spindlewood, 70 Lynhurst Avenue,
Barnstaple Devon EX31 2HY

Cover illustration by John Hurford

ISBN 0-907349-86-2

A catalogue record for this book is available from
the British Library.

Typeset by Chris Fayers, Woodford, Cornwall EX23 9JD
Printed and bound in Great Britain by
Short Run Press Ltd., Exeter

To Jean

Chapter 1

The dark blue Ford Transit van moved steadily towards its target. It was late, but not so late that a van with back windows blackened would attract attention. As it swung from Birch Lane into what remained of the partly-demolished Buxton Road, its headlights illuminated a giant billboard that had been erected on waste ground:

> HEDLEY GILMORE
> AND
> THE DELIVERANCE PARTY
> OF GREAT BRITAIN
> FOR A FUTURE YOU CAN TRUST

Above the corner store, the last bedroom light was switched off. The van pulled up outside in the poorly-lit street. The occupants waited while a Mini full of young people drove past quickly. The driver kept the engine running. A burly man in overalls and a black balaclava jumped out of the back doors.

The Mini was well down the street before Araf was able to make Imran stop. There was something suspicious about that van. The road was narrow. Imran started to make a very slow and clumsy three-point turn, the first since he had passed his driving test. Araf twisted round in the passenger seat. Imran couldn't find the reverse gear. Araf saw a small flame arc towards the window from the man's hand and then the explosion. Imran brought his foot off the clutch too quickly and stalled the Mini on the last stage of the turn. Araf swore at him. The van sped away.

J J Pickles stared at the mirror. Yes, they'd been right to fuss. She looked at the traffic-stopping colour of her cheeks – "As if you're wearing rouge, Joanna Jane" DON'T CALL ME THAT! – and at her luscious red lips! The blood transfusion had changed her completely. Well, it had changed her *complexion* completely and brought an avalanche of vampire jokes down on her:

> *Have you made your coffin this morning, Joanna Jane?*
> DON'T CALL ME THAT!
> *Fangs for coming around.*
> *We've only got Ribena. D'you think you could pretend this once?*

Ha, bloody ha: she was fed up with them. Even her best friend – her ex-best friend – Maggie, had called wearing a huge crucifix and a string of garlic round her neck.

Her diet was the problem, the parents, doctors and teachers said, and it had taken the dizzy spell and faint in P.E. to make her see sense. Vegetables just aren't enough. "Bugger," thought J J. She wasn't going to give up without a fight. The body needs meat, they said, and the milkman can't deliver a pinta blooda day along with the semi-skimmed.

What hadn't changed was J J's single-mindedness, the determination she brought to everything she did: an *awkward, feisty young woman* was how her Year Eight Form Tutor had described J J and she had tried to live up to that praise ever since. She wasn't going to eat meat. The experts could find her a balanced diet without meat that would give her enough iron or whatever it was that was missing.

J J laced up her DM's. Twelve holes and she'd told her

10

mother at least fourteen. She wondered whether to wear black or black with a touch of grey. Play safe. J J put on her black leggings, a black *Cure* T-shirt and a well-holed and frayed black woollen jacket. The sleeves hung down over her hands; a *little-girl-lost* look. "Anything but," thought J J, and took it off again. It was going to be a hot day.

"You're a disgrace, Joanna Jane." DON'T CALL ME THAT! "No boy'll look at you."

"Perhaps that's the idea, Mum."

"Don't be silly."

"Boys don't have to be the only thing on a girl's mind."

"I know that, but it's only natural."

J J lifted one of her mother's magazines and flicked through the pages. "Make-up and stupid fashions and sex. Look at them: everybody posing; nobody real. That's not natural. I mean, look at them; a load of daft tarts."

"That's not a polite word, Joanna Jane."

"We're Northerners, Mother; everybody says *daft*. And DON'T CALL ME THAT!"

* * * * *

Rashid Hassan looked in the bathroom mirror and combed his hair: *hybrid; cross; half-breed; half-caste; mongrel; Eurasian*… Not long ago he'd known the Thesaurus entry off by heart, but now there were a few he couldn't remember.

Their terraced house was small, a mill-worker's house built last century. His parents' breakfast-time conversation penetrated the bathroom.

"It will work out, Ellen."

"The interest, Farouk, will cripple us. We can't afford another loan."

"There is a new scheme; short-term; very favourable terms. I'll go see the manager."

"You're not facing facts."

"If people paid what they owed us…"

"If… if… We can't live on *ifs*, Farouk."

This was not a good time to ask for money to buy those jeans from Top Notch. "Why not something from the stall?" his father would say. "Have something from the stall, or is what your parents sell not good enough for you?"

Rashid – neat dresser, neat speaker – always wanted to answer: "Frankly, father, no, it isn't," but never did. He kept quiet. His father got angry and said it was just a matter of names, designer labels, but Rashid knew different. Style, quality *and* the right names: that's what he wanted, and they weren't to be bought on his parents' market stall. There, you found only jeans with names nobody had ever heard of and shirts from Far East countries nobody had ever heard of. Rashid respected and didn't want to hurt his parents but… well… he had standards to maintain. He splashed more water on his hair.

"What about Tahir?"

"What about him?"

"Go and see him. He'll help."

"After all the speeches he's made about us, and about how I've denied my culture, deserted my community?"

Rashid used his hands to flick back the hair that fell from his middle parting on to his forehead. A NOWT: that wasn't in the Thesaurus but that was Brancaster's favourite word for him; neither black nor white: a right bloody *nowt*. Rashid fastened his shirt; a right good-looking bloody *nowt*.

* * * * * *

Michael Brady wriggled his long, thin body out of the sleeping bag fully dressed, pushed his lank black hair from his eyes, and raised his head furtively over the window sill. The sky was beginning to lighten and, over the top of the large sign GILMORE PROPERTY SERVICES, he saw the city centre streets, Westgate, York, St John's, wakening to another working day. A gang of cleaners was leaving the supermarket and a delivery van, emergency lights winking, was being unloaded outside a clothing store. Over the brow of the hill at the top of York Street, he could just see the roofs of the indoor markets. He wondered if his mother was worrying where he was; wondered if she was at home or somewhere with her new boyfriend. He knew his dad wouldn't be bothered: "'E's fifteen, nearly sixteen; a big lad; can learn to look after 'imself". The office was only on the third floor of Churchill Tower, but the view began to blur and move and he felt dizzy. He pulled back quickly from the window.

It wasn't really running away. They knew he didn't go far and they never reported it to the police. It was as if an agreement had been made without any words being said.

For Michael, it was having a break. Other lads of his age went camping with the scouts or stayed at relatives' or friends' houses. None of that was on offer for Michael, so he made his own *breaks* especially when his parents' arguments got too much.

They knew he'd be back. Two nights away at the most: a bit of breathing space; no harm done. Churchill Tower had been empty for over a year. This was the third time Michael had slept there and each time, he made sure that he left early in the morning before the security guards arrived to make the last of their casual patrols.

* * * * *

Four hours later, on what had become a bright May morning, Monday of the mid-term holiday, Michael walked along Birch Lane, the long, busy road that led from the edge of the city's commercial centre into the dense knot of terraced streets where most of Brancaster's Asians lived. Just off the centre, the large stone buildings that had been mills and warehouses were either empty or part-occupied as furnishing or wholesale fabric shops.

> ON THIS SITE STOOD GRANGE MILL
> BUILT IN 1798
> AS THE FIRST STEAM-POWERED MILL
> IN BRANCASTER

I LOVE YOU SHAHZEERA

Gaps where some had been demolished revealed a patchwork of back lanes and gerry-built brick outbuildings with corrugated asbestos roofs and shaky iron fire-escapes. The boarded windows of empty buildings were plastered with posters and grafitti:

GOD'S POWER
POWER
POWER
POWER
TO HEAL YOU TODAY
SET YOU FREE FROM YOUR HABITS
TO DO MIRACLES IN YOUR LIFE

Could do with a miracle or two, thought Michael.

I LOVE YOU SHAHZEERA

THE DELIVERANCE PARTY OF
GREAT BRITAIN –
THE TRUTH IN BLACK AND WHITE

I LOVE YOU SHAHZEERA

Michael found Rashid and J J standing on Buxton Road opposite the fire-bombed corner store. Groups of people had gathered on both sides of the street. He felt uncomfortable in that part of the city. Twice he'd been threatened and almost beaten up by a gang of Asian boys. The fire-bombings and beatings had made things much worse: people were angry; they wanted action. Michael was frightened, shaky. He shouldn't have come.

Inside the building, fire officers were checking to see

that nothing was still smouldering, while outside, one policeman was interviewing distraught members of the family and others were trying to calm a crowd of angry neighbours. Rashid was taking photographs.

Michael flicked his hair from his eyes and glanced nervously about. On a grey, plastic drainpipe behind him:

I LOVE YOU SHAHZEERA

The crowd moved from the road as a large Mercedes drew up. The driver jumped out and opened the passenger door for his boss. A short, stout, dapper man in his forties stepped out and made his way across to the family.

J J asked Rashid if it was his Uncle Tahir. Rashid seemed reluctant to answer and did not stop taking photographs.

"Could be," was all he replied.

Across the road, Tahir offered sympathy to all the family and gave a bundle of money to the extremely grateful father.

Michael was asking J J and Rashid if they could go somewhere else when Araf and his gang entered the street, all dressed in their uniform of battle fatigue trousers, black vests and red headbands. They saw Michael and charged, all except Araf and Imran, his right-hand man. Before J J could stop him, Michael ran.

"Brereton Moor this afternoon," J J shouted after him. Rashid hoped Michael hadn't heard. Why did she want Michael with them? He hardly said anything, or did anything except depress everyone around him. And he was beginning to smell. Rashid had never seen him in

16

anything but that hideous *Iron Maiden* T-shirt. Perhaps J J just didn't want to be alone with him.

Araf put his hand over Rashid's camera lens but spoke to J J, "Enjoying yourself?"

"Don't be stupid."

"Your friends 'ad a nice bonfire last night."

"They're not my friends." J J pulled Araf's hand away from the camera. "That's expensive equipment. Keep your hands off."

"Tell your friends…"

"They're not my friends, stupid!"

Rashid thought she had gone too far this time and waited for the explosion. Araf could be very nasty. He was eighteen, older than the boys who followed him about. He bullied them and no one ever answered him back. A two inch scar curled just under his right eye, a monorail of crude stitching and a testimony, many believed, to a vicious knife fight. Araf's mother, whose heart still skipped when she remembered hearing the scream and finding her little boy surrounded by a broken milk bottle, knew otherwise. Araf looked hard at J J for a moment and chewed his gum open-mouthed. Then he sneered as if she wasn't worth answering.

"Taking photographs won't stop 'em, Rashid."

Rashid wanted to stand up to Araf as well, but held back the words. He gave a soft cough, a habit he had as if he was giving himself time to shape his words more precisely, "It's for school; a project."

"Projects won't, either."

Rashid opened the camera and removed the used film. He didn't answer. He saw Imran watching him closely and gave a nervous flick of his head in greeting. Imran

17

nodded and smiled back.

"I suppose you know how to stop them, do you?" said J J.

Araf continued to ignore her. "You've got strange friends, Rashid. Soon, you'll 'ave to decide 'ose side you're on."

The others in the gang returned from chasing Michael unsuccessfully. As he walked off with them, Araf shouted, "Decision-time!" over his shoulder, "Tomorrow afternoon, Simpson's Mill."

J J tried to catch Rashid's eye, "He's not talking about cricket practice is he?"

Rashid fiddled at putting a new film into the camera. He usually managed this deftly, without any trouble, but this time, he was fumbling and J J noticed. "Don't let friend Araf get to you. He's all talk."

"He's not my friend!" Rashid snapped, "And he's not getting to me!"

"Great: nobody's anybody's friend this morning." J J smiled: "Comb your hair."

"No."

"Go on. It'll do you good. I'll hold your camera."

Rashid smiled in return and handed her the camera. He turned, looked at his reflection in the shop window and with long strokes, tidied his jet-black hair. Just like the Fonz, Rashid stood with his legs well-apart and slightly bent at the knees to do this. J J wondered how it helped.

The fire-engine was pulling way. The family walked down the street and into a neighbour's house. Rashid pocketed his comb.

"Bet that feels better," said J J. "Come on, let's go and

18

find Michael."

J J walked off in the direction Michael had taken. Rashid hesitated, looked in the opposite direction towards Araf's gang but then followed J J.

★ ★ ★ ★ ★

Damn! The first shot had missed. Obersturmbannführer Scheffler had seen the small puff of rock-dust as it hit just to the left of the prisoner. That shot haunted him. He was proud of many things in his life. Among them were his well-developed, healthy body; his alert, clear-thinking mind; his unwavering dedication to the cause, and his prowess with a variety of weapons, particularly the hunting rifle. He had done better with a crossbow a few days earlier. True, the prisoner had to be finished off by a guard but that was a failing of the weapon used at that distance and not his prowess.

The second shot had hit its target and killed the prisoner instantly, but the first still haunted him fifty years on. Carelessness and unfinished business had cost him and his comrades dearly. He swivelled in the armchair and faced his companion. As he spoke, he stroked his chin.

"He knows me, Gilmore. He is the one person who can, without doubt, identify me. You know what to do."

Chapter 2

J J let her hand drift along the tips of the hedgerow's branches as she freewheeled down the gently inclining road. Brereton Moor was one of her favourite places and visiting it always made her realise that Brancaster wasn't a bad place to live; a biggish city, but not so big that half-an-hour's steady bike ride wouldn't bring you into open countryside.

Rashid was already at the bottom locking a chain around his expensive French racing bicycle and looking for a good hiding-place. He was annoyed. He never felt at ease in the countryside and avoided contact with it as much as possible, believing it was a sure source of allergies, colds, dirt and silly thoughts about flowers and animals. And, on top of that, there was the third party; the gloomy gooseberry. J J pulled up alongside and Michael, whose ancient Hercules (found in a skip) had no brakes, jumped off and pulled to a stop fifteen metres beyond.

First, J J wanted photographs of a dilapidated dry-stone wall that went halfway up the moorside. Rashid started to take the shots, but couldn't see the point.

"They're for my art project."

Rashid cleared his throat: "They are walls, simply walls!"

"Nothing's 'simply' anything. Look at the beautiful patterns in the stone and that stuff that grows on them."

"Lichen," said Michael quietly.

After the wall, they walked steadily towards Hangman's Rocks, a popular spot at weekends for

Brancastrians. When they reached the old quarry and the tumble of huge boulders beneath it, Rashid was panting and sweating heavily. J J wasn't sympathetic. "You should have left the leather jacket, Rash. It is summer, you know."

"I shouldn't have come. I'm allergic to countryside."

Michael was chewing some bilberry leaves, "You catch things? Colds 'n that?"

Rashid answered him sharply, "I just don't like it. I like concrete and tarmac. You know where you are with them."

"You're talking out of the back of your 501's, Rashid," pronounced J J.

"No, I'm not! If I get hungry out here, what am I supposed to do? I don't see a McDonald's. If it starts to rain…"

"It's not going to."

"And cities are cleaner."

"Brancaster clean!"

"The grass doesn't fool me, J J. There's dirt everywhere here! This place *is* dirt."

"I'll get it removed before we come again, Rash, and sprayed with air freshener."

"And it's boring."

Michael spat the mush of leaves from his mouth and said quietly, "It's not!"

J J held her arms out to embrace the landscape: "How can you get bored with all this around you?" She scrambled up the side of the quarry and stood looking over the sheer cliff face created by this huge bite into the hillside. Rashid followed her slowly, anxious not to rip or dirty his clothes. Michael stayed below. He knew what would happen if he climbed to the top and looked over. He sat and read the rocks like the chapters of a history book. Some pages were neatly and deeply carved:

E.M. LANCASTER 1st XXIV FOOT
1882

PVTE. THOMPSON IGGLESTONE
1917

TO GEORGE, B.E.F. 1940.

Later pages, *PAUL + DEBS; SCOTT 4 JULIE; DARREN 4 WENDY; NIGE*, were lightly scratched on the cleanly cut rock faces. Shahzeera's admirer had been there as well with an aerosol paint spray.

With the great expanse of the moor behind them, J J and Rashid took in the scene: in the middle-distance, Brancaster's sprawling streets and buildings, with two new housing estates stretching like stubby legs to the south, had the rough shape of a giant dozing in the warm afternoon. Rashid took a couple of shots. To their right they saw the narrow road they had followed twisting and rising from the Birch Lane district and running along the foot of the moor past a single isolated farm labourer's cottage. There was no traffic. Commuters, avoiding the clogged main roads, used it to go and come from work, but for the rest of the day it was quiet. Rashid attached a powerful zoom-lens to his camera and took more photographs.

"I don't want farmhouses."

"I want to take back some proof of civilisation."

A dark blue van entered the frame of Rashid's viewfinder and stopped just before reaching the farmhouse. Three men jumped out of the back and the van was driven on to the farmhouse. It stopped again, a woman stepped down from the driver's seat and lifted the bonnet. Rashid kept taking photographs until J J told him to stop wasting film.

"What else do you want?"

"Some close-ups of the rocks; the texture; fissures, colours."

"Not much colour."

"There is if you want to see it."

"I hope I'm going to be credited for this in your project."

"Neon lights over the main school entrance, Rash. Now, come on, take some photographs. We've still got the old mine to do."

They dropped halfway back down the moorside and walked along a sheep track that etched an uneven contour through the heather and bracken and two rocky ghylls towards the short adit. Michael, unsmiling, still dragged his feet in the rear, but Rashid had taken his jacket off. The old mine was little more than a shallow, partially flooded cave. Well-rusted Coke cans littered the entrance. Few people came there. Two hundred metres down the slope, a dense coppice bristled in what was, otherwise, an almost treeless landscape. Beyond the wood and now blocked from their view was the farm labourer's cottage.

Rashid refused to go into the cave and told J J she'd have to be satisfied with photographs of the entrance.

"For lead; never used," said Michael.

"There could be thingies, Rash, on the roof; stalagmites," argued J J.

"*Stalactites*," corrected Michael, hesitantly. The other two waited. "Tights…" he blushed. "Tights… come down."

"Whatever they are, I want some shots of them."

"There's none."

Rashid was curious: "How come you know so much about this place?"

Michael shrugged his shoulders. J J answered, "Probably another one of his lodgings: *spacious, well-ventilated room with magnificent views and running water, down all the walls. Neighbours extremely friendly and covered all over with wool.*"

Rashid smiled but Michael turned away and looked down at the coppice. J J came up quietly to his side: "A joke, Michael. Ve haf vays off making you laff, you know."

Michael knew the cue and muttered: "But, whatever you do…"

J J finished the sentence, "… don't mention ze vor!" and broke into a John Cleese imitation, giving a stiff-arm salute, kicking her legs high and placing a finger under her nose for a moustache. At last, Michael smiled, but shyly, as if he was uncomfortable with expressing himself in this way. J J put her hands on his shoulders and in another of her voices, a plummy, P.G. Wodehouse one, said, "You've always got us, old fruit, your faithful and enterprising friends."

This time, the smile was a comfortable one. Michael knocked J J's hands away and raced off making great

25

bounds through the bracken down to the wood: "You'll never take me alive!"

JJ started off after him, then stopped and turned back to Rashid. He was angry. He hadn't liked seeing her hands on Michael's shoulders. "I'm certainly not running," he said. JJ nodded in sympathy, "It'd mess your hair, wouldn't it?"

Suddenly, Michael was alive and enjoying the day with his friends. With a big smile on his face, he turned and sprayed JJ with imaginary machine-gun fire as she entered the wood. JJ took a bullet in the shoulder, stopped, and staggered backwards. She recovered quickly, dropped to the ground and started returning Michael's fire. Rashid ambled up behind her with his jacket slung over his shoulder and she shouted for him to get down as well. Rashid grimaced and, making sure the grass wasn't damp, sat carefully behind a tree. This wasn't the romantic walk with JJ that he'd hoped for. He shaped a gun with his hand and pointed it unenthusiastically in what he thought was Michael's direction.

"Bang! Bang!"

Michael had moved. Ducking low, his mind full of his nine-year-old days when organising the next game was his only worry in the world, he ran off the path to the right and to the edge of the wood where he dropped to the ground, and used his elbows to edge forward into a small, dense thicket of blackthorn.

JJ saw a slight depression in the earth twenty yards ahead. Zig-zagging, she ran forward and jumped into this natural *foxhole*. No firing from Michael. He mustn't have seen her. JJ studied the trees and bushes to find out where he was. There was no movement, but she suspected he'd gone into the thicket on the right and was waiting for them to pass it. Then he'd spring an ambush. That's what she'd do.

Behind her, there was a lot of movement and a lot of noise. J J gestured for Rashid to join her and when he did, told him to be quieter and to "outflank" Michael.

"Talk English."

"He's in those bushes. Move round the side of them."

Rashid climbed gingerly out of the hole, put his hands in the air and shouted that he wanted to surrender. Michael and J J started making their gutteral gun-noises again and, before he realised what he was doing, Rashid had dropped to the ground.

"I'm as stupid as they are!"

It was ridiculous; he'd never played *soldiers* when he was younger. Nevertheless, to humour the other two, he ran forward crouching low. Behind him, a fierce fire-fight raged.

"What am I supposed to do when I get there anyway? She's not getting me to crawl in those bushes; definitely not."

An odd bulge in the earth at the side of thicket tripped him. He surveyed the damage: bright grass stains on both sleeves of his white shirt and a hand on his Nike Air trainers. Rashid shivered with horror; it was a hand. He stood up quickly and shouted to the others, "There's a body!"

Michael burst out of the bushes still firing his machine-gun, "I know. It's yours. I shot you when you

27

ran over there."

"I mean a real body!"

Playfulness drained from them. Michael pulled away some of the grass and ferns that crudely camouflaged what they had found: a frail, elderly man who looked, from the blood and bruises on his head, as if he had been badly beaten. J J gently brushed sandy earth from the man's face and Michael lifted his limp wrist.

"He's not dead."

Children, we must stay here in the tunnel until they have gone. An hour, a day, a week – shush, Miriam, shush – I don't know. We must be very quiet… No, Leo, the dog will be all right. They don't want your dog… Leo, you mustn't go back out… Leo!

The eyelids flickered and then the old man spluttered and spat dirt from his mouth.

J J told Rashid to go to the farmhouse. "Get some help. Telephone the ambulance and police."

Michael suddenly found his hand gripped firmly. The old man shook his head and spoke faintly, "No… no one. My house. Get me to *my* house." Rashid hesitated. There was something very compelling in the old man's simple, faint plea. The accent was odd; a comical mixture: Europe somewhere, West Yorkshire, and somewhere else. Michael said they shouldn't move him because he might have broken bones, but the old man pleaded once more. Being very careful, they half-carried, half-dragged him out of the wood and across the road.

The front door was wide open and they stepped

along a lobby, past one locked door to a roughly-furnished living room with a stone-flagged floor. They lowered him gently into a well-used, lumpy armchair. J J's eyes searched the room for signs of who the man was: the walls, the table, the mantelpiece were bare; there were no mementoes; no photographs of his family. The place felt barren and cold; a shelter, not a home.

"A fall, that's all," he muttered, gasping for breath. J J shook her head at the others and mouthed, "A fall," incredulously. The old man didn't want them to do anything except see to the fox. He was worried about the fox, "Vixen... young... shot... the fox." That's why he had been in the wood. He had been going to feed the fox when he... when he had fallen.

Michael found the young fox not far from where he had hidden in the thicket. It was thin and spindly-legged, and instead of the sleek redness Michael expected, its coat was dull and coarse. The old man had made a door from wood and chicken wire which penned the creature into a natural shelter provided by large stones half-embedded in the earth. Close by, Michael found several tins of dog food and a tin-opener.

The old man nodded and came close to smiling when Michael returned and told him that the fox was all right. Two long strands of his dark hair, still thick and thinning only slightly on top, fell down his face. J J brushed them back. She wanted to get an ambulance and the police: "You didn't fall."

The old man tried to get out of the chair but fell back. His breathing was fast and noisy. He gripped the left side of his chest as he spoke, "No police; no anyone!"

JJ didn't want to promise, but let Rashid and Michael persuade her since it looked as if the old man was going to make himself much worse if she didn't. They all promised not to go to the police or to involve anyone else. He'd be all right. They could check on him the following day. JJ asked questions. What was his name? Where did his accent come from? How long had he lived there? And she told him he was daft not to go to hospital. The old man said nothing. He stared ahead and, attempting a gesture of dismissal, waved his hand weakly. Rashid told JJ to leave him alone. She didn't. Who'd beaten him up? Why wouldn't he go to the hospital?

"You must have family. We could get in touch. Tell them you're not well."

The old man broke his silence and spoke slowly, "Dead. All dead, a long time ago. All."

"You *were* beaten up, weren't you?"

He gripped the chair arms so tightly that his knuckles whitened, "Not your business! Now get out! I never asked for your help."

Chapter 3

The items on the late evening news broadcast were drifting through her consciousness without registering. J J shivered with tiredness and pulled herself from the armchair. In the front room, she heard the persistent, irritating *tock, tock* of her mother still typing at the computer keyboard. Established only a year, the Pickles Executive Search Agency (*You would be in a right pickle without us!*) was a success.

"The morphological features; that is, facial characteristics are identical…"

J J pressed a button on the remote control to turn the television off. The picture darkened. She held another down and the colours became garish. She was very tired. She crossed the room to switch off at the set. The first-ever trial in Britain of an alleged World War Two criminal was being reported. Is the accused, Hans Bauer, really the person the prosecution claims he is, the vicious SS camp officer, Franz Scheffler, or is it a case of mistaken identity? A still of the accused man came on to the screen. J J stopped and studied the photograph. In the head-and-shoulders shot, the seventy-six year old looked startled. His closely cropped head and jug-handle ears brought about a confused reaction in J J of amusement and pity. He looked… weak and… *haunted*, perhaps by the terrible things he had done. His look reminded her of the old man they had helped that afternoon. He had that same look. People hiding from others? People with something to hide?

That photograph was followed by another from 1942 of the SS Officer. J J couldn't see any resemblance but an expert on how the body and bones grow had testified that Bauer and Scheffler were the same person.

After that, they showed archive footage of Auschwitz. J J remembered the old man's accent and what he had said about his family: "Dead. All dead, a long time ago".

"They should leave those people alone after all this time." J J's mother had entered the room.

"No, they shouldn't. If they did wrong, they should be punished. It doesn't matter how long ago it was."

Margaret Pickles thumbed through the sheaf of computer paper she was carrying. "Even British Telecom are inquiring about us now."

J J went to bed and fell asleep with the war trial, the grainy film of the concentration camp and their discovery of the old man weaving irregular, disturbing patterns in her mind.

* * * * *

Farouk Hassan had not been sure about the darkroom and the expensive cameras. "It could just be another of those things he picks up one minute and drops the next. And it won't be cheap."

It hadn't been. Rashid was in there now processing the negatives of the films he'd shot during the day. It was true that Rashid had picked up and put down several hobbies and sports, but two he held very close: photography and cricket.

He worked steadily and efficiently: developer, stop-bath, fixer: the bombed-out shop, the crowd, the firemen for himself; the walls, Hangman's Rocks, the cave for J J's project; the landscapes and farm cottage for anyone who wanted them. For almost a year, he'd had his darkroom and in that time he had never had an accident of any kind, not so much as a water mark on a negative. He was very proud of the expensive equipment he had persuaded his father to buy. Like his bedroom and like his appearance, the room was neat, well-kept. Rashid washed and dried the negatives. He'd make contact prints the following day and ask J J which she wanted enlarged.

Before he left the darkroom, Rashid took a strip of bright red cloth from a drawer and tied it about his head. He looked at himself in the small mirror on the wall next to his enlarger. He hadn't tied the knot tight enough and the headband slipped down over his eyes.

* * * * *

Michael knew where to find his Dad. He always went to The Lion after the gun club on Monday evenings. Michael didn't want to talk to him. His father always went on about him ducking school, wasting his life, not caring about his parents, not helping around the home; about his mother's boyfriend; about Asians taking all the jobs... It went on and on, sometimes ending with him hitting Michael. It was much worse since he'd lost his job; as if he'd been made redundant so that he could concentrate on being bitter towards everyone. Michael didn't want to talk; he just wanted to see him, see his Dad, that's all.

It was late evening and the streets still seemed dazed by the heat of the day. A dog, eager to rest but unable to, lay on the flagstones, its chest heaving and its tongue lolling out of the side of its mouth. A family played cards on their front step.

Michael found a smiling crescent of clear glass in a stained-glass window. Bob Brady was sitting with friends close to the bar. At one end of the large, crowded room, tables were draped with union jacks and a Deliverance Party meeting was taking place. A speaker, sharply dressed in a black suit and grey tie, referred to the high unemployment figures, blamed them on immigrants and called for repatriation. Everyone at Bob Brady's table cheered and clapped.

"Strike a chord, Bob? How long's it been now, a year?"

"One year, three months and eighteen days."

"You interested?"

Normally, Bob hated direct questions like this that cornered you about your politics, but he was convinced that what the speaker was saying was true.

"Suppose so. Never been very political, mind."

Jake Gillery, a paunchy forty-four-year-old with sideburns and a shard of someone's tooth in his knuckle, both relics of his Sixties youth, pushed a leaflet across the table.

"You know what's what, and you know this country's being took over by foreigners." Bob nodded in agreement. "This lot…" continued Jake, gesturing towards the speaker, "are down to earth, speak *our* language. And this lot don't just talk."

Stepping around drinkers who had spilled outside, Michael went up the entrance steps and hovered; a quick word, that's all; try to get some money. A couple of young men with bare arms and shaven heads pushed past him and went inside. Noise from the interior fizzed outside momentarily: clinking glass; the hubbub of conversation and the speaker's words, "Proper little Uriah Heeps when

34

they first started coming over. Wringing their hands; ever so 'umble in their corner shops. But now, look at them swaggering, acting as if they own the streets, own the towns!"

Bob clapped furiously at this, his hands above his head. Jake called across, "Might be something going down our place."

"Turner's Garage? I'm no mechanic."

"Nothing special like; stores, driving, that kind of thing. Interested?"

"Could be. Beggars can't be choosers."

"You've got the right qualifications."

Bob took a long drink. "What's them?"

"You think the same as the rest of us down there about what's 'appening to this country and you want to do something about it."

Jake scribbled a telephone number on a scrap of paper. "Ask for Avril. Drink?" Bob nodded his head and then studied the number.

From the door, Michael saw his father take the piece of paper and put it in the top pocket of his jacket. He patted the pocket twice, a mannerism he had, and Michael felt a sudden shiver of loneliness. He wanted to go home and decided to wait outside for his Dad.

Half an hour later, Bob Brady and his friends left The Lion. None of them got into cars. All of them walked, almost marched, in the general direction of Birch Lane. Michael pushed his bike after them. They didn't have to go far. Michael saw the man before they did. He watched the others, and then, hesitantly, his father, break into a trot; watched the isolated man stand paralysed. Michael turned his back, mounted his bike and peddled quickly away.

35

Runnin'… almost fallin'… "Come on, Bob!"… teenager again… like after them dances at Methodist Hall… 'anging round afterwards… no girl… all spots… tekkin' on Dewsbury lot; out… out of puff; norras fit as… then.

Put the boot in like all the others. You do, don't you? I mean, you're poppin', aren't you? Feel great. Adrenalin or whatever's racin' and you just want to do it. And you've 'ad a few drinks. And it's to do with your mates, innit? Initiation, Jake said. Group 88 or summat. And it's about solidarity, loyalty, Three Musketeers, what 'ave you, blood-brothers like, but not your blood: 'e's a foreigner, a Paki and anyway, it wasn't 'is 'ead. I'd've known if it was. Different feel. I went for 'is shoulder. Not kickin' 'eads. And anyway, these shoes 're soft not like the ones Jake and the others were wearin'.

What was 'e doing walkin' round there that time o' night? Askin' for it.

★ ★ ★ ★ ★

It was a clear night crowded with faint, coltish breezes. Leo Meyer was in the armchair where the young people had left him. He could not move his arms or legs. Opening his eyes was like lifting huge tombstones. Through the window he saw the great hogback outline of the moor and the trees of the wood like the risen dead, the branches their arms held upwards in supplication, the trembling leaves their futile, whispered pleadings.

Barking, disturbing the peace in the middle of Plac Zgody, the Place of Peace. Stupid dog. Pleased, so pleased to see me. Leaping. Wanting to lick my face. No time. Cross the square. Emptied ghetto lanes. Past the pharmacy. Emptied ghetto houses. Past the saddler's, the emptied orphanage. Trucks nearby. Soldiers running. Shots. Nearly there. Children's screams. Duck low, scramble into our burrow, the dog safe, me seen, family sacrificed.

He remembered his family and intoned their names in his mind. His memory sought for summer scenes to bring his father, mother, brothers, little Miriam, the aunts, uncles, cousins, all of them and so many back to life, but was confronted and chilled by the darkness of that constant winter of fifty years ago and the guilt of his survival. His bones, his flesh felt like water. He willed death to come so that he might, at last, be reunited with those he loved, but his call was not answered.

He thought of the young people who had helped him and felt contrite for having spoken so harshly to them. He could so easily have warmed to their lively presence in his lonely house, been cheered by company he had isolated himself from for many years. But it was right to get rid of them. Friendship with him would place the young people in great danger.

Chapter 4

Rashid didn't mind the early rise to help his father load the van, but breakfast and the drive to the lock-up had been very quiet and he could sense a lecture coming to the boil: growing up; respect for women; respect for your elders; belief in God; respect for women; clean body, clean mind; respect for women; being a responsible citizen; not following everything on television and in the magazines, especially all that sex; respect for women, etcetera. Farouk had a lot of serious talks with his son.

Marrying Ellen Barnes had caused a rift with his family and, although Farouk knew he had made the right choice, he often felt uneasy about having to bring the boy up outside the cultural security of Brancaster's closely-knit Asian community. That community was a living handbook on what to do and say to children; parents, with plenty of help from others, worked their way through the pages. Farouk could be very critical of the narrow-minded and intolerant attitudes found in some chapters, but envied the ease that it gave parents. It was much harder to bring a child up without that support. Farouk regretted not being able to confirm Rashid in some of the ways of doing things that he had been brought up with; in family ritual that was central to occasions such as deaths and births, and also to everyday happenings such as mealtimes, greetings and prayers. The talks were his way of trying to compensate.

Rashid kept quiet and tolerated these sessions. He respected his father as a good man and a loving father and as someone who had had to make a very difficult decision to cut himself off from people and things he held dear.

He also knew that he talked a lot of sense. He just wished he wouldn't go on so much.

Rashid opened the double-garage doors and his father backed the van as close as he could. Rashid started to load black work-boots with reinforced toes into the van but Farouk stopped him.

"Leave those. Somebody wants them all; a special order."

Rashid replaced them inside the garage. As they worked, Farouk talked, "Work hard at school, Rashid. Get good qualifications and then you won't have to get up before everyone else to load vans. Education. And don't stay round here. There's too many things'll pull you down. There's things that are all right round here, like, but there's more opportunities away. They'll always put a label on you round here."

Farouk bent to break open a box, "Put these shirts in." He stood upright for a moment and frowned at his son. "That school report wasn't good, Rashid."

"Big fat B's," thought Rashid. "That's not bad!"

"You're going to have to pull your socks up." Farouk wanted to see A's in Rashid's GCSE results. A's would help convince him further that the path he had taken when he married Ellen was the right one.

"You don't seem to be bothered. You don't seem to know the meaning of hard work. You wouldn't believe what I had to do when I was your age." He stopped and waited for an answer from Rashid.

"After I've helped you set up the stall, Dad, can I go round to my friend's?"

Farouk lowered the blue overalls he was about to carry to the van and looked hard at his son. Was he listening at all, this, his only child? There had been complications at his birth and Ellen couldn't have any more children. A punishment one relative had told him. Maybe he was too soft with the boy; maybe these man-to-man talks were wasted on him. Farouk tried to suppress the idea, but sometimes he thought his son was shallow, only interested in his appearance and enjoying himself. Look at the fuss he made over his clothes; flash, expensive. Look at how he's dressed to help load the van! The costly white polo shirt (not much under twenty pounds) and the stone-coloured, washed cotton trousers! Look at the way he acted, as if money went off if it wasn't spent on the day you got it. Ellen always defended him, "He'll be all right. Just give him time."

Time was something Farouk was short of. Debts and anxiety were piling. "Things are difficult, Rashid. This VAT business is killing me."

Rashid wasn't sure what he could do. Definitely not ask for the jeans from Top Notch. He went to the front of the van and waited while his father tidied up.

Imran walked by the backs of the houses opposite. He shouted to Rashid, "You comin' this afternoon; Simpson's Mill?"

"Maybe," was all Rashid replied.

Farouk locked the garage doors and climbed into the van. Rashid got into the passenger seat.

"You seeing that girl?"

"And some others."

Farouk's face creased as if he was trying to work out a very difficult tax calculation. The engine was running fast and he was having difficulty finding first gear. It clunked into place.

"Always treat women with respect."

"Not much chance to do anything else," thought Rashid.

The old van rattled its way from the back street on to Birch Lane and towards the city centre market.

★ ★ ★ ★ ★

Still in her pyjamas, J J padded through the front room-cum-office towards the kitchen. She could have gone to the kitchen by the hall, but always made this morning ritual detour to greet her parents. They were both behind computers, her mother gazing at the VDU but her father on the telephone.

J J's mother did not deflect her gaze and in her monotone delivered the token weekend and holiday-time greeting: "Doing anything nice today, Joanna Jane?"

DON'T CALL ME THAT! Over her mother's shoulder, J J saw Rashid walking slowly up the drive to the house.

"Thought I'd strip off, borrow a high-powered telescopic rifle, climb to the top of the town hall and..." Here, she mimed the action – *soldiers – that wood – wonder how the old man is?* "spray a few innocent citizens with intensive fire."

Margaret Pickles prodded one – two – three letters on the computer keyboard and pressed ENTER.

"We've had an inquiry from Bulgaria of all places."

J J's father covered the telephone mouthpiece and spoke to his wife, "Could we manage a full analysis – Morning, Joanna Jane – for Bayliss and his lot by the middle of next week?"

"Should think so."

He uncovered the mouthpiece, "No problem, Ted."

J J continued her walk to the kitchen, "Then I'll jump!"

The walk up the long, curving drive of Spring House always made Rashid feel uncomfortable and defenceless – a *Treasure Island* pirate who had climbed the stockade and was approaching the log-house. That was the last book he'd read right through and he half-expected the windows of Spring House to bristle with muskets. The openness had something to do with it; snooker table lawns to the right and left of the asphalt and no trees except for one laburnum heavy with blossom.

Someone was watching him approach. The curtain in the ground floor left bay window moved slightly. Margaret Pickles, unarmed, let very few occurrences interrupt her work. This boy's visits to the house was one of them. She watched him combing his hair as he walked the last few steps.

Rashid was still groping for the bell among the tangles of clematis when J J, dressed in black leggings and sagging T-shirt, opened the door.

"Don't look so frightened, Rash."

"I'm not! It's just… I don't know… different here."

J J put on an American accent, "You're just marrying me to get out of the ghetto, ain'tcha?"

"No, what I really want is your wardrobe."

She grinned. "The old man's place? See how he is?"

Rashid nodded. "What about Michael? You'll want your precious Michael to come along, won't you?"

Now she was a southern belle from *Gone with the Wind*:

"Forget him, Ra..ahsheed. He… he means nothing to me now, honeychile."

Rashid sighed. She was in one of those moods. And she could be very funny, but when, deep down, you felt attracted to her as Rashid did, it was very irritating, because you couldn't communicate. You could never say serious things when she was like this. Everything was turned to a joke. And Rashid wanted to say serious things – not exceptionally HEAVY things – but he definitely wanted to get closer to J J.

★ ★ ★ ★ ★

Bob Brady was in a bad mood when the doorbell rang. You needed to wear a suit for an interview so he'd spent an hour trying to iron some shape back into the one suit he had. He hadn't worn it since he had been best man at his brother's wedding in 1977, the year when brown was in, and it had been lying on the floor of the wardrobe since then. The first chance he'd had of a job for ages and he was going to be late and wearing a suit that looked as if it had been tumble-dried in a skip.

To make matters worse, the posh girl had one of Brancaster's dusky brethren with her. Bob snaked his paisley patterned tie under his collar and wondered if this Asian wandered about late at night.

"Whah?"

"We've come for Michael."

Bob Brady fumbled with the ends of his tie. "I'm only his father; 'ow should I know where he is? Does what he likes, that one." He slipped the tie knot tight. Rashid looked Michael's dad up and down. The problem must be

44

genetic. He wondered if there were any mirrors in the Brady flat.

"Very nice," said J J.

Bob Brady looked at her hard. "You tryin' to be funny?"

"Not at all. Coming back in, that look."

Bob Brady pointed to the road, "And 'er too. She's another one does what she likes."

Julia Brady was getting out of a BMW. The driver, a very smartly dressed, tallish man, younger than Julia, came round from the driver's side and walked with her towards the flat. Julia, still in her nurse's uniform, saw the group at the door and stopped halfway up the path. She kissed Simon and told him she would see him that evening. He looked towards Bob, shrugged as if he wished things were different, and then returned to his car.

"Michael not here?"

"Money, fancy car and a suit; do you fine that, won't it?"

Julia tried to ignore her husband and to smile at the young people. He persisted, "Sooner you clear off with precious Simon, the better."

"It's not as simple as that. What's the suit for?"

"Interview. Turner's. The big garage."

Rashid stared after Simon and the car. Simon had been wearing an Armani suit!

J J elbowed him, "We're off." Stage policeman's voice – she really pushed her luck. "And rest assured Mr and Mrs Brady, when, not *if*, but *when* we find your son, we'll let you know."

★ ★ ★ ★ ★

Turner's Garage was on Herse Road, a busy section of the city ring road which was only half a mile from a motorway entry. Not so far from Birch Lane, thought Imran; just a short drive and several routes to choose from in a maze of steep terraces and small industrial developments. Imran was sure it was the place. Employees had been seen at Deliverance Party rallies.

Not long after midday, apart from the petrol pumps at the front, the place seemed deserted. Trying to look confident, Imran walked across the road and round the side of the building to the Service and Spares Reception area. The pump attendant gazed into the corner of his booth and shook his head as another English wicket fell in the one-day international.

Imran was breathing heavily. This was silly. He was doing nothing wrong and he could be wanting to fix up a service for the Mini. The door to Reception was locked. Imran walked on, calling "Hello," but not too loudly. At the back of the building, he found two large loading bays but the overhead doors for each had been pulled down and locked. On the access road at the back and on the waste ground beyond, there was nothing to confirm his suspicions: a Mondeo with a new exhaust and a badly dented Peugeot awaiting repair.

There was a slight gap at the bottom of one of the bay doors. Imran knelt and looked under. All he saw was a badly oil-stained floor and the tyres and lower front of one vehicle. Imran pressed the side of his face against the tarmac to get a better look. The vehicle was blue and could be a Ford Transit.

For a burly man, Jake Gillery could move very quickly and quietly. He was standing over Imran as he started to get up.

"Now then, you're a fair way off the reservation today, Geronimo." And then with mock politeness, "May I do you the service of directing you back to your teepee?"

Imran rose and dusted the knees of his jeans, all the while thinking of an excuse for being where he was. There were four in all, but only three in mechanics' overalls. The other one, tall, stooping, with a Zapata moustache, was wearing an elderly crumpled, brown suit with wide lapels and slightly flared trousers. Imran grinned broadly and acted as if he was slow-witted. That usually helped.

"Eh, I was told there was a place that sells tyres, retreads, round 'ere. For a Mini, like."

"Nothing like that here. You were told wrong."

"Sorry, mate."

One of them repeated what Imran had said, mimicking his accent. Jake pushed his face close to Imran's, "I'm no mate of yours, Geronimo. Now get off this property."

Imran turned and walked away without saying anything. It wasn't until he was clear of the garage and in among the more familiar streets off Birch Lane, that he realised his shirt was soaked with sweat. He decided not to say anything to Araf. Araf would do something stupid.

Chapter 5

J J was about to knock on the cottage door, when Michael stepped out from behind a tangle of bramble at the side of the house.

"Stayed on guard, like, through night… and mornin'. Thought they… you know, the ones who brayed him, might come back."

The house was cold, hidden from the sun for most of the day by Brereton Moor. The old man had slumped off the armchair into a kneeling position on the floor with his arms, pinned by the chair sides, pointing grotesquely upwards. His mouth hung open and a thin line of spittle snailed its way from one corner down his chin.

Rashid and Michael drew him gently back into the armchair. Michael pulled the bottom of his T-shirt up and dabbed among the salt-and-pepper bristle until the old man's chin was dry. His complexion was grey-yellow, like a page of newspaper left in the sun. He muttered something they couldn't make out and, though his eyes were shut, his thickly-haired eyebrows lifted and fell rapidly. He was worse than the day before. J J bent close to him and heard a steady rattling in his chest.

Leo Meyer opened his eyes. He tried once more to wave the children away; to get them out of his life. *Stupid; interfering*. Their features bulged, distorted as if he was looking in a fairground mirror. *There is a girl, yes, a girl. Little Miriam? Is it? Dark eyes we all knew would make men's feelings spin. And mother? Is mother here? Both so thin. Not much more work left in them. Father? Father at the special work, the oh-so-special fixing, sealing, making everything airtight. Father, artisan, proud of his work, even in that place.*

"He's very hot."

The room; mustn't go in the room. Not their history. Dead.

J J bustled and started to give orders. They had to be practical. Warm the place up and get some food into the old man. In the pokey kitchen, she found an almost bare pantry; one half-full bowl of goo furred with mould and one unopened tin of chicken soup. Choosing wasn't going to be a problem. Now, matches for the gas.

Michael pulled bits of pocket-fluff from what remained of a chocolate bar and tried to get the old man to take some of it. The old man looked at him quizzically and waved him away. Michael told him the fox was all right, but wasn't sure he understood.

Rashid had never done it before and it was very messy, but he managed to light a fire. He found a store of kindling in a small outhouse; bleached, twisted twigs and roots of heather like a pile of bones. The flames had a fierce hunger on them and devoured Rashid's first offerings rapidly. He piled more on and the blaze stirred the old man. He grunted and spoke.

"The only way out," he said, "is the chimney."

Rashid and Michael nodded and smiled at him. A single tear worked its way, stopping, starting, down the old man's left cheek. J J banged and cursed in the kitchen as she searched damp-spotted cupboards and grimy shelves for a clean pan to heat the soup in. Michael shrugged his shoulders at Rashid; he wasn't sure what else they could do. He squatted on the stone floor close to the crackling fire. Rashid turned away to explore other parts of the house.

Stairs from the lobby led to one long attic bedroom. Like below, this room was strangely empty of clutter, of evidence of homemaking and comfort. There was a single bed, a large metal trunk full of old blankets, and a tallboy. A rope had been strung across the room and, dangling from it on hangers, were a jacket and two pairs of trousers. Rashid pulled out the drawers of the tallboy carefully, one by one. They were empty except for the top two which held the old man's underwear and his few shirts which Rashid with admiration saw had been folded with meticulous precision. He looked at his watch and remembered Araf, Imran and Simpson's Mill.

Back downstairs, he found that the first room off the lobby was still locked. Almost automatically, Rashid stood on a stool that was conveniently near, and swept his hand along the door lintel. That was where he kept his darkroom key. Leo Meyer's key fell to the floor.

The curtains were closed inside the room, but a faint light penetrated the thin material. The only furniture was one dining chair and, on the floor beside it, an elderly, loaded, reel-to-reel tape recorder. In the dim light, he thought the wallpaper was peeling, but when he walked around the room he saw the walls were covered with yellow, curling papers crudely tacked to the plaster. All of them were concerned with the Nazi concentration camps: magazine interviews; photographs – hideous tangles of emaciated bodies – torn from books; statistics; newspaper articles on the pursuit and trials of war criminals in South America, France and Israel.

On the floor, close by the tape recorder, was a cutting that hadn't faded. Only ten days old, it was a report from *The Guardian* on the war crimes trial and a photograph of the accused. Someone had inked a cross on his face and written, *NO!* They had pressed so firmly that the paper was torn.

Rashid felt nervous. He knew that he had invaded a place that was sacred to the old man. Nevertheless, he wanted to know more. He pressed the large start button on the recorder. It clicked loudly. At high volume, a man spoke in German, his voice pumping like pistons on hard consonants.

Rashid knew the voice from somewhere: a video in a history lesson; finely manicured rows and rows of soldiers slicing the air and the twentieth century with that salute. Why did the old man listen to this stuff?

"Aaargh!" It was the old man.

The voice from the recorder startled everyone in the living room and the old man's body jerked violently spilling the bowl of soup J J was trying to spoonfeed him from. Michael tried to calm him while J J ran through to where Rashid was and played the recorder buttons like a mad pianist until the reels stopped turning.

"Idiot!"

"Don't call me that!"

"He went mental in there when he heard this."

"Yeh, well, perhaps that's because he has something to hide."

"Meaning?"

"You heard who it was. Why should anyone want to listen to recordings of Hitler unless they were some kind of Nazi? And look at all this."

"I'm looking!" A large sheet with a series of symbols drawn on it caught her eye:

TRIANGLE RED   – POLITICAL
TRIANGLE GREEN   – CRIMINALS

TRIANGLE PINK	- HOMOSEXUALS
TRIANGLE BLACK	- PROSTITUTES
TRIANGLE VIOLET	- CLERGY
STAR OF DAVID YELLOW	- JEWS

People collected things, all kinds of strange objects from photos of their favourite pop stars to the contents of ancient latrines found on archaelogical digs. The old man collected information on Nazi concentration camps. So what? But even as she said this to herself, J J was trying to make connections between the evidence of the old man's obsession, the beating he had received and the news report she had watched the evening before. She looked at the cuttings on the walls and snatched the one Rashid handed her. It was all getting too complicated.

"He could have been a prisoner."

"You'd want to forget if you'd been in those places, not keep all these things."

"Nazis! Trials! Concentration camps! God, it's holiday, we're off school; you fancy me; I fancy you. What's happening?"

Michael was crouching by the window when J J and Rashid returned to the living room. The old man was breathing hard and whimpering.

"There's a car going past dead slow outside."

"Oh, no!" J J was still angry and still arguing with herself that there were easy answers, "Another one who's paranoid."

"The driver's looking at the house."

Making no attempt to hide herself, J J crossed towards the window. "Going slow and looking at houses. Evil."

"Red; a Sierra."

"Stop him then! He can take the old man to hospital."

Before JJ could reach the window, Michael stood up and grabbed her by the arm, "Don't. He could be the one who tried to kill him yesterday."

"Kill? Let's look for simple explanations first, Michael."

Almost tripping over the old man's legs in his haste, Rashid joined them and told Michael to let go of JJ's arm. JJ was grimacing. Michael looked puzzled, as if he hadn't realised what he had done and how tightly he was holding her. He released his grip. There were white blotches on her flesh where his fingers had been. Michael studied his offending hand.

"Sorry."

Although Michael was taller by several inches, Rashid pushed up against him and warned him never to do that again. JJ grinned and told him not to be so stupid, "Fight over me later boys. But stop that car now."

Michael, still embarrassed by what he'd done, turned quickly back to the window. The car had gone.

Rashid had had enough. So he was stupid, was he? He was an idiot. Stupid because he wanted to help her, protect her. He had had enough and wanted out of that miserable place and away from that drooling old man who was probably some nasty Nazi who should have been locked away years ago. She'd said he could have been a prisoner. Well, there was a way of finding out if that was true. The Nazis had marked them all.

When JJ and Michael turned form the window, they saw Rashid rolling back one of the old man's shirt sleeves. The old man's hands fluttered feebly in token resistance.

"They had numbers tattooed on them; the prisoners in those camps."

JJ stopped him. "We're going to help him because he needs our help, Rash, not because of who he is."

"I'm not helping a Nazi."

"What if he's a Jew? Some of your friends down Birch Street aren't too fond of Jews, are they?"

Rashid stayed calm. "They're not my friends."

"Roll that sleeve up and you'll lose this friend."

Rashid let go of the old man's wrist. It fell limply over the chair arm. "Forbidden… room… forbidden," he muttered. Rashid and JJ locked gazes. Michael, keeping his eyes low, shuffled past them saying he was going to get his mother. She would get the old man to hospital.

Rashid objected, "He doesn't want to go to hospital," but Michael went quickly out of the door and ran to the wood to get his bicycle.

"Sometimes people have to be made to do things for their own good, Rashid."

Rashid didn't reply. He was fed up. Hitler probably said things like that. Now, with the old man exhausted, beginning to doze fitfully, and with Michael gone, he ought to have been happy. It was an opportunity to spend some time alone with JJ. Rashid realised he didn't want to. The bossy JJ really put him off. He headed for the back of the house to get more firewood. As he did, he looked at his watch again.

"Don't forget your appointment with your friends," JJ called to his back.

Rashid stopped.

"Cricket practice, isn't it, at Simpson's Mill?"

Rashid didn't turn around. He had been undecided, wanting to keep his options open. Had things been different; had JJ been in a less bossy and sarcastic mood;

had she shown a glimmer of affection towards him to back up her statement that she fancied him, without doubt, he would have put all thoughts of Simpson's Mill out of his mind. Now, he was determined to meet Araf.

"I said I'd help Dad pack up at the market."

There was a pause. Then J J sniggered. Rashid bit his lower lip. Respect for women? How could you respect one who knew you were fond of her and yet treated you like this?

J J abruptly stopped laughing and shouted angrily, "Araf's lot're almost as bad as the heroes who're throwing petrol bombs."

Rashid still didn't turn around. He was not going to argue with her and was not going to give her the satisfaction of seeing that he too was furious. "No, they're not," was all he said and left the house, not to fetch firewood, but to go back to Brancaster.

J J ran to the door and shouted after him, "I'll be all right on my own – don't worry. If they come back to try to kill him again… I'll… I'll…" J J spluttered to a halt. She had thrown those words after Rashid as a joke. She knew the old man had been beaten up, but had told herself that it had been casual violence; some city idiots not much older than herself who had got a sick thrill out of kicking an old man around when they hadn't found anything of value in the house. As she watched Rashid, one hand on the handlebars, the other pushing hair from his eyes, cycle steadily up the road away from the cottage, J J realised that she now believed Michael's explanation: someone did want to kill the old man.

Back inside the cottage, J J returned to the *forbidden room* hoping it would provide an answer. The photographs should have appalled her, but didn't. Perhaps it was because she had seen ones like them on television – once having to wrestle with her mother to keep the documentary on since Margaret Pickles did not think it was suitable viewing – and in history books. It was the statistics that shocked her, that made the scalp at the back of her head tingle.

BIRKENHAU: four additional modern crematoria with multiple ovens were installed and began to operate during the period March – June, 1943, increasing the capacity for the disposal of bodies at Auschwitz to:
4756 per day
33,292 per week
142,680 per month
1,712,160 per year.

J J left the room, locking it behind her. In the living room, the old man was sleeping. Gently, she rolled back his shirt sleeves. There was no tattooed number.

Chapter 6

"Great, our Michael's here and great, he wants me to drive to Brereton Moor and help some old man. And great, I'll be out of the flat and away from The Moaner, the self-centred so-and-so of a husband who's angry because I laughed when I saw him in that suit and didn't do cartwheels when he said he had a job."

Fifteen months before, Julia Brady might have done just that; fifteen months before, getting a job might have made a difference, might have stopped him slipping into such a swamp of self-pity and anger directed at everyone near him, and stopped her walking away from their marriage. Right, he had a job. Julia Brady genuinely hoped that it would help him turn a corner, point his life in a new, happier direction, but she knew for certain that she wouldn't be by his side whatever happened. Thirty-four; attractive; with her own income and with Simon Leighton, a catch by anyone's standards, Julia had made her mind up.

And he'd got stuck into Michael! "Where've you been?" (As if he cared!) "Who is this old guy? How d'you know he's been beaten up? You should keep your nose out of things like that. Who knows what the old guy's been up to. Hanging around with that Asian'll get you into trouble." No wonder the lad stays away from home.

One quick look at the old man told Julia that he ought to be in hospital. He was weak and from the sound of his breathing, his lungs were badly congested. With Michael's help, she made Leo Meyer as comfortable as possible on the back seat of her Morris Minor, the car she and Bob had bought to take them touring the Scottish Highlands on their honeymoon, a car loaded with happy memories. The old man was conscious of what was happening, but had either accepted that it was for the best or was too weak to protest.

J J waved them off and was bending to pick up her bicycle when a red car drove past, following the Bradys and heading towards Brancaster. She ran to the bottom of the small, neglected front garden and saw that it was a Sierra (or what she thought was a Sierra – she wasn't very good on cars) and that it had a badly dented driver's door. He's been somewhere and now he's coming back, she thought. It was a coincidence, and nothing more.

Michael's mother shouldn't have gone through the old man's wallet. He was somebody who was ill. Why did they have to know he was Leo Meyer? Why did they have to know he was sixty-four? Why did they have to know he was Jewish? If they let him stay anonymous, it would be harder for his enemies to find him. Julia Brady, brusquely efficient in her place of work, had shaken her head at this silliness. Simon Leighton, her boyfriend, dashing to a meeting of Hospital Trust Finance Officers, kissing Julia quickly, had also been very sceptical about the story Michael told – murder? concentration camps? – but had congratulated him on his caring attitude.

"More of that's needed in our society. Well done, Michael."

Hiding in the small bathroom attached to Leo Meyer's bedroom in the intensive care ward, Michael studied the veins on the inside of his arm just below the elbow. How did they do it? Get needles and tubes in there? At first, the feeling which these thoughts induced was similar to that he experienced when he touched velvet or heard chalk squeaking on the blackboard, a momentary shudder of revulsion. Rubber tubes on bunsen burners; the hose pipe on the outside tap. The feeling became much worse; his stomach was queasy; he started to faint. Gripping the side of the sink with one hand, Michael bent down so that his head was between his legs. He hated everything to do with hospitals. The only time he had been in one until that day was at his birth. He couldn't watch them on television and hadn't even visited his Dad after the car accident. Coming into Brancaster General with his mother and Leo Meyer had taken a lot of courage. Staying was going to take a lot more.

The queasiness was going, but Michael knew it was bound to come again when he left the bathroom and saw what the doctors and nurses had been doing to the old man; what all the swishing, clinking, wheeling and muttering really meant. He took a deep breath and listened. They had all gone, including his mother, and clearly, had forgotten about him.

Sure enough, when he stepped into Leo Meyer's bedroom and saw a dripfeed tube snaking under a bandage into the old man's arm – no tattoos – Michael's stomach began to somersault once more. He breathed deeply again, clenched his fists and looked down. The veins on his arms bulged with the tension. He forced himself to look elsewhere. He had to get over it or else he would be no good as a guard. And the old man had no one else.

★ ★ ★ ★ ★

Some said Simpson's Mill should be pulled down before it fell down. Others said it was an important testimonial in stone to Brancaster's great industrial past and should be preserved.

Rashid wondered why he was there. Was it because he was tired of his status as a *nowt* and wanted to belong to one particular group, one tribe? Was it the need to take sides? For a long time, such thoughts had never troubled him. Apart from puzzlement over the odd nasty word in the playground, Rashid believed he had grown up in *one* community. He had white and Asian friends; they messed about in sandpits together, stayed at each other's houses, ate each other's food. Something had changed in recent years but Rashid wasn't sure whether it was to do with feelings on the streets of Brancaster or with his growing up. Perhaps he had become more sensitive to divisions that had always been there but that his childhood had sheltered him from. Whichever it was, he knew that, at times, he felt he belonged to neither the white nor the Asian community, that he was in a no-man's land, caught in the crossfire of taunts and rejection.

Rashid wasn't sure why he was at Simpson's Mill. Perhaps it was a need to get out of that no-man's land; perhaps he just wanted to get Araf off his back; perhaps it was anger with J J. She shouldn't have spoken to him in the way she did. Anyway, there were much better looking girls around. And just about every other girl was better dressed. Rashid tried to think what it was that he liked about J J. It wasn't her hair. Her hair was… fair. You couldn't say too much about it: fair, dirty-blonde, shoulder length, centre-parting, unremarkable. Nowhere near as attractive in Rashid's eyes as the richly dark hair of the Asian girls. Her face? Pretty, but too long and thin for Rashid's liking. It was like her figure (not that he knew much about that, well-hidden as it was under the shapeless clothes she wore); it lacked the gentle, softly overweight roundness he liked so much in many of the local Asian girls.

It should have scurried away as he approached but didn't. It took its time, edging forward with short, alert jerks of its head. A rat? Rashid didn't know. He stopped and waited until it disappeared somewhere along the sunken drain that ran the length of the building. He shivered; the early evening was very warm and bright, but the large yard at the back of the mill was, as ever, dank and dark. The entry to Araf's HQ was hidden by a pile of bricks and rubble, a boarded window to what was once an office in the huge abandoned mill. Rashid stepped gingerly through the rubbish dumped in the yard but couldn't avoid skidding on the sodden remains of several mail order catalogues and falling heavily on his backside. Rashid stood, straightened his red headband and strained to see the damage: the thick, damp, furry moss that covered most of the asphalt had marked his trousers badly.

"The Nowt's messed his pants!"

Araf's companions, five in number, laughed dutifully. Rashid was nervous but smiled to himself when he saw Araf swaggering towards him. The gang leader was all shrugs and twitches and grunts, a poor imitation of the latest Hollywood B-movie brat-hero. He walked slowly towards Rashid, short, hands in his pockets, a bouncy attempt at a Big-Man's-walk, his shoulders swaying from side to side. Rashid pulled a pulpy mass of glossy catalogue pages from his trainer:

He wondered what J J was doing; wondered if she was with that headcase, Michael.

Araf was alongside him. He pulled repeatedly at his crotch like a kid who needs the toilet, "Glad you could make it, Nowt." Twitch of the arms, shrug, twitch of the head, point. "Sorry about the trousers."

Rashid nodded. He just wanted to get on with it, with whatever they did when they gathered at the mill.

"Please step into my office, Mr 'assan."

One of the boys jemmied the window-boards free with a large screwdriver and they all climbed into Araf's "office". Araf took centre stage, the only one allowed to sit on the one piece of furniture, a rotting leatherette sofa. Rashid stepped through the papers that littered the floor, the spillage of filing cabinets removed years before; facts and figures on production at the mill and on the history of the woollen industry:

> *... long ago as 1840 there was exhibited at Leeds a beautifully distinct facsimile of the will of Louis the sixteenth, entirely woven by the Jacquard machine. Since then, its powers...*

Imran stood to the right of the sofa, straight-backed, arms folded, stern expression forced on to his long, normally friendly face. Rashid caught his eye and got a weak, half-apologetic smile in return. Imran was older than he was, but Rashid remembered half-burying him in Brately Road Playschool sandpit when they were toddlers. Fixed to the wall behind his old friend was an enlarged street map of the Birch Lane district. Coloured pins marked where recent fire-bombings and beatings had taken place. The others in the gang also stood erect about the cold, damp room. "Everyone wants to play soldiers," thought Rashid.

Even sitting, Araf twitched. "It's like them or us now, 'assan."

The others nodded like puppets.

"No in-between. Know what I'm saying?"

Araf stretched his arms along the back of the sofa. "We're not going to sit around and take it, 'assan."

The trousers would have to be soaked as soon as he got in; that green stuff was hard to get out. "What's this got to do with me?"

"You don't 'ang around with us as much as you used to, and you're a *nowt*, and you've got white friends. We're not sure we can trust you."

His mother had a stick of that magic stain remover somewhere. "It's not like that and this is st... stu..." Rashid stopped himself. He didn't want to make Araf angry. The polo shirt had cost more than the twenty pounds his father thought it had.

Araf jumped to his feet and poked Rashid repeatedly in the chest, "When they start bombing and knifing us, it's like that all right. We're the new Jews and what's 'appening now is another 'olocaust. OK?"

This wasn't the first time Rashid had heard this argument. His father, Farouk, had said that it wasn't true. Bad things were happening but one couldn't compare what had come out of Germany in the 1940's and what was happening in Britain today. To do so was to insult those who died at the hands of the Nazis. Rashid kept quiet. It was better just to let Araf spout.

"But we're not going to let 'em push us around. We're going to 'it back."

Rashid looked about the room, anywhere except at Araf's snarling face. By a door that led to the rest of the old mill building, he saw a milk crate full of bottles. They contained a pale pink liquid and the necks were stuffed with strips of rag. Rashid looked at Imran. Imran turned from his gaze and shifted his feet uneasily.

Araf barked, "In or out, 'assan. Make up your mind. And make it up by tomorrow, cos we've got things to do."

Chapter 7

"Whatever you do, Leo, do it well."

"Yes, father."

"He wants you at his house."

"Why, father?"

"Work: what else? His personal servant."

"Yes, father."

"While we are able to work, Leo, in this camp, we are of some use to them."

"Yes, father. But what is the new work you are doing, father?"

"Building. Old farmhouses – renovating them."

"Why?"

"How should I know?"

But we knew, father, didn't we?

No one had come to see the old man. It was nearly eight o'clock, the end of visiting time. Michael had sneaked from the *en suite* bathroom and along to the large, busy reception area to get something to eat. It was a good time to do it. Visitors were streaming along all the main artery corridors that led from the numerous wards to the main entrance. On his way back to Leo's room, if stopped, he could be a visitor who had left something by a relative's bedside and was going back to retrieve it.

The snack dispenser kept rejecting Michael's money. Nearby, a wall-mounted speaker relayed a programme from Radio Brancaster; a phone-in. The politician, Hedley Gilmore, was telling an Asian caller that it was nonsense to suggest that, as leader of the Deliverance Party, he would support *ethnic cleansing* in any way, shape or form.

However, what I do know is that the multi-racial society does not work; mixing does not work. It destroys cultures. Aren't you proud of the culture and traditions which you have inherited? Wouldn't you like to see them preserved?

Michael tried another combination of coins. His mother would be back on duty now. He didn't want her to see him. Forget about the snack. Through the large glass doors at main entrance, he saw a long queue of cars waiting at the hospital junction to slip into the city centre traffic. The egg mayonnaise sandwiches dropped.

No, I am not, strictly speaking, asserting that one race is superior to another. What I am saying is that the races are different, have different aptitudes, ways of living and so on, and as such, develop better when apart – a simple, commonsense way of looking at things.

Michael needn't have worried about being stopped by anyone. Brancaster General was a huge, busy hospital, a dense cluster of Victorian buildings which was constantly being adapted by the addition of annexes, walkways and partitioning walls. Visitors were still coming out of the wards as he walked along the corridor to Intensive Care. Past wards 23, 24, 25 named after dead council worthies, Oldroyd, Cockshott and Micklethwaite, across the glass-pannelled walkway, a left turn and he was back outside Leo's quiet refuge. The corridors were all right; he was used to them now and if he didn't think too much about where he was, he didn't feel queasy. Leo's room and the tubes, and the charts, and the old man's vulnerable body looking so small, so worn out and fit for nothing else but sleep, was different. Michael stopped for a moment outside the door and took a deep breath. He heard someone coming across the walkway; the same tread he had heard several times that afternoon; Staff Nurse Trimble. He pushed the door gently and saw a tall, angular man, with thick, black curly hair bending over Leo. A doctor? No white coat. He could still be a doctor. The man twisted Leo's head as if he wanted to get a better look at him and his other hand gripped the tube that was dripping new strength back into the old man's body. Doctors didn't hold patients' faces like that!

Michael's fear vanished. Leo Meyer had to be protected. He pushed the door wide and ran at the man. His rush was wild. The man turned, said something that the furious Michael couldn't make out, and before the boy could get a grip, winded him with a stiff fingered jab to his solar plexus. Michael fought for breath and to stay upright but the man forced his head down as if he didn't want Michael to get a good look at him. Michael tried to swing his fists at the man – trousers heavy, worn, dark blue, not summer wear, a couple of inches short, stains, an archipelago of stains about the flies – but the blow seemed to have drained his strength. The man pushed his head lower and said something else. A foreign accent? "Sorry." Another voice. Someone else was in the room.

The man pushed Michael to the floor and ran for the door. Simon Leighton did not try to stop him. He stood to one side and committed a picture of the man to his memory.

Simon quickly checked that Leo Meyer was all right, then buzzed for a nurse and helped Michael to his feet.

He asked if he had any idea who the man was. Michael was still finding it hard to breathe.

"Be… one of… them that beat 'im… up."

"You actually saw Mr Meyer being beaten up? You'd recognise the men?"

Michael shook his head, "Just found 'im."

"He could have had a very bad fall."

Michael couldn't believe what he was hearing. "They tried to kill 'im!"

Simon smiled and put his hand on Michael's shoulder, "You've been at the videos again, Michael. Don't let your imagination run away with you."

Michael shrugged the hand off. He wasn't sure about Simon. He just seemed too young, too cool-headed, too well-heeled, too ambitious for his mother. He made a fuss of Mum and she was happy, but Michael couldn't see him staying with her.

"Look, you've brought him to hospital. We'll take it from here. You go on home."

"He's no relatives. I want to stay with 'im."

That smile again, adult, "understanding", annoying, "Well, it's a nice idea, Michael, but you can't. He's safe here."

"What about 'im who's just been in?"

"We get all kinds wandering in here. Most of them are harmless. But, don't worry, I'll get security on to it. Now, go home."

A smiling, pale nurse entered and expressed surprise at seeing Mr. Leighton there. Simon told her they had had an intruder and that she should check the patient and alert security. He would give them a full description of the man.

The nurse busied herself with Leo, and Simon led Michael into the corridor and across the walkway.

"The police will sort everything out."

Michael told him how upset the old man had been at the cottage when they had mentioned the police. Simon stopped. He had to go through Oldroyd Ward to his office.

"Living on his own... getting on. People can act strange. It's great that you're concerned, really, but don't overdo it."

Michael nodded and kept going towards the main entrance. Simon called after him. "Your mother does worry, Michael." Without breaking his stride, Michael half-turned and nodded again.

* * * * *

Rashid remembered the headband as soon as he saw J J waiting for him outside his house. He snatched it off but she had noticed. "No comment," was all she said, and then surprised him by kissing his cheek and then, gently, his lips. Rashid said nothing and didn't respond. It was too public, too close to the house. He didn't like the way she had taken the initiative again, and he was very confused about how he really felt. J J broke the silence.

"Want to do those prints?"

Farouk and Ellen liked J J but they weren't too pleased to see her that evening. Their talk had inevitably come round again to money and Ellen had told Farouk that he had to go and see his brother, Tahir, about a loan. If he didn't, then she would.

In the darkroom, Rashid worked by his orange

safelight to make the contact prints. When he had finished, J J studied them through a jeweller's eye-glass to choose the ones she wanted enlarged. She surprised Rashid by indicating several of the shots he had taken of the cottage from Hangman's Rocks.

"I thought you wanted stones and textures."

"Can you blow them up so that we can get a better look at the people jumping out of that van?"

"No problem. But I don't know if they'll be good enough to recognise them by."

"They're the ones who beat up the old man."

"So you really do believe someone's after him?"

J J stepped closer, "You didn't like me kissing you outside, did you?"

Rashid backed into the sink. J J had no sense of time and place and she was so forward. He really wasn't sure he liked that in a girl. "I could start on the blow-ups now."

J J smiled. She was enjoying making him uncomfortable. "Or you could start on me."

"Rashid!" His mother knocked on the door. "Can I come in?"

Rashid switched his safe light off and the whitelight on. "Of course, Mum."

There was a telephone call for J J. It was Michael. J J's mother had said she might be at *that Asian boy's*. Michael told J J what had happened at the hospital and about his worries that the man in the dark blue suit might try something again. J J told him not to worry and that now they had some evidence.

The beans were fast-forming a solid, burnt mass in the pan when Michael put the telephone down and returned to the small kitchen in his parents' flat. If he had remembered to turn the grill on, his toast would have been burnt as well.

"Something's burning!" his dad called helpfully from the living room settee, as Michael excavated the mess his supper had become and dolloped it on to a plate.

Coming to stay at home that night had been an easy decision to make. It meant he still had contact with the hospital through his mother. Michael had left a note at reception asking her to check regularly on Leo. In the morning when she came off her night shift, she would bring him news of the old man.

Michael joined his father in front of the television in the living room. *News at Ten* was on and Brancaster was being talked about: increase in racist attacks, heightened tension in the community.

"I gorra job today."

"Great."

Michael's father nodded towards the television. A mainly Asian protest march down Birch Lane to City Hall was being shown.

"One of the few that lot 'aven't taken from us. Start tomorrow."

Michael said nothing. He never liked to confront such issues in his own mind. Maybe his dad had a point. There were only so many jobs to go around. But then a teacher at school had told the class that we'd been glad to see the Asians and West Indians when they first started coming to live in Britain. Michael didn't know and didn't want to think about it.

"They shouldn't let 'em do that. Tek over t' streets."

Michael picked a blackened pan-scraping from his

mouth and muttered that there was nothing wrong with them doing that.

"They're foreigners," Bob answered sharply, as if that scotched any argument that Michael might be thinking of starting.

Michael felt himself getting hot and uncomfortable. Usually, he would keep his head down and agree with anything his dad said. Bob Brady had always bullied his son, at times physically – hard slaps about the head – and every day, verbally, brow-beating him about his appearance, his laziness, his failures on the sports field and in the classroom, his lack of ambition. Michael had learned never to invite such bullying but what had happened to Leo Meyer at his cottage and in the hospital had brought about a change. Michael didn't understand why. Perhaps it was something to do with Leo's odd accent, perhaps it was to do with Michael's own feeling of being different, of being in a minority, of being bullied.

"They're not foreigners."

Bob ignored him, "Askin' for trouble, they are."

"What are they supposed to do? Let their 'omes get burned down?"

The news had moved on to the cricket one-day international. His dad still turned out in the odd friendly fixture for their local club's fourth XI. Michael hoped the report would stifle any retort he wanted to make to his son's defence of "our coloured friends". It didn't. Bob Brady was angry; bloody angry. A ray of happiness had shone into his life, and, after fifteen months, he had a job – nothing special; not his trade – but a job, and could his family share in this happiness with him? Could they hell as like. He turned from the television and faced his son.

74

"What d'you know about it, all of a sudden?"

Michael attempted a disarming comment on England's miserable performance at Old Trafford.

"You know nowt, so say nowt." He looked at the television again but Michael could see he was building up a head of steam for a longer attack on his son's ignorance.

"And who does your Asian friend support when it comes to cricket internationals? Eh? Eh? All that stupid chanting. Where do 'is loyalties really lie?"

Michael took his plate into the kitchen. Rashid had played two games for Yorkshire Under-15's. He looked out of the window and thought of the injured fox penned among those stones with only just enough room to turn.

"Most of their money goes back to Pakistan, you know!"

Its leg was mending well.

"And they treat their women like slaves! No rights at all!"

Michael pictured himself pulling Leo's makeshift door down and setting the young fox free into the thick, welcoming darkness about Brereton Moor.

★ ★ ★ ★ ★

Nelson Avenue, a row of large detached Victorian houses once owned by mill managers, points a crooked finger north from Birch Lane towards Brereton Moor. The largest house on the row is the Asian Cultural Centre. Several of the protest march organisers were standing outside arguing about how effective such events are, when a snub-fronted blue van moved slowly down the opposite side of the road. An attractive woman, dressed as if returning from an expensive restaurant meal, was in the passenger seat. She shook her head and the driver accelerated past the Centre. Someone in the back cursed and banged his fist hard against the wheel arch.

Stretches of Birch Lane were still busy in the aftermath of the march. The bombers sought and found a secondary target on a quiet back street.

The sound was familiar to Imran; that dull crump. He had heard it two nights before when he hadn't been able to turn the Mini round fast enough. He sprinted to the corner and caught a glimpse of the blue van as it sped through the network of alleys away from Birch Lane towards Herse Road and Turner's Garage.

Chapter 8

None of Farouk's stock could be saved. The morning after the bombing, the Chief Fire Officer thought he was saying the right thing when he told Farouk he would send him a report to go with his insurance claim. Farouk forced himself to smile and thank the man. The premiums were expensive. It was two years since he had last renewed the insurance on the lock-up.

Ellen Hassan watched her husband closely, a good man, a hard-working man, and a man whose gentleness had meant so much to her when they had first met. He wasn't like the other boys she'd gone out with, image-conscious, one-track minded immaturities, who wanted to maul her as soon as they were alone. Farouk was polite and sensitive to what Ellen wanted. He said that he was happy just to be in her company and he meant it. He respected women and believed that the relationship between a man and a woman was uniquely created by God for love and for children. Ellen's friends found him and his views funny, quaint, not listed on the contents pages of their magazines. Ellen was impressed. The physical side of their relationship grew gradually, gently. Farouk never tried to force intimacy, never attempted the cheap male bribery of, "If you really love me, then…" He respected women: he loved Ellen, loved her enough to break with the cherished traditions and disciplines of the community he also loved.

As she watched Farouk pointlessly turning over charred, sodden stock with a spade, Ellen wondered if this was the last straw; if her husband was going to break under the strain of all their debts. She had never seen him so low. Something had to be done. Ellen called Farouk out of the ruins of the lock-up and told him that she needed to get away for a few hours and was going to visit her sister in Otley. Farouk said that was a good idea. There wasn't much she could do at the lock-up and, with their stock destroyed, they couldn't open the market stall. He would try to see a few of their creditors. They might be sympathetic when they heard about the fire and give him more time to repay. Ellen nodded but she knew that sympathetic words were all Farouk would get from such visits.

Rashid couldn't understand his father's reaction. Why didn't he get angry? Why was he still behaving in such a calm, reasonable, "Everything will be fine; everything will work out," manner? Rashid was angry. He wanted to lash out. What had his Dad's calm, reasonable manner got him apart from debt and derision?

Rashid wasn't sure why he had brought JJ and Michael to see the damage. They were more interested in that old man. Perhaps it was because he wanted to show them something that, despite his mixed blood, he considered to be uniquely part of his experience of living in Brancaster. Perhaps despite his dislike of Araf and his stupid posing, Rashid believed there was something right in what that bully was saying and doing. Perhaps he wanted to show JJ and Michael the mess their type were making, and, as with puppies, rub their noses in it.

Their type? Rashid reined in his charging thoughts. So the Nowt, of all people, was defining *types* now, was he? Rashid allowed himself a slight smile and looked at his friends. Michael, head down, hair curtaining most of his profile, was kicking a foot against a pile of ruined shirts and looking, as always, as if he was guilty of most of the crimes committed locally. J J, in contrast, was striding through the puddles, examining anything that was left as if she was going to find all the answers to Brancaster's racial problems. "Individuals, not types," Rashid told himself and then shouted at whoever had started the fire, "Stupid racists!"

When Michael stopped his kicking and agreed, Rashid realised his anger hadn't diminished and needed a victim.

"Stupid racists like your father!"

Michael shook his head but said nothing.

"He hates Asians."

Michael was only half-listening to Rashid. Other voices were demanding his attention. He heard Araf and his gang before he saw them and shifted his stance to be ready to run. "He doesn't. He just… gets the wrong ideas."

Araf and his gang came round the corner at the same time as J J emerged from a great clump of rose bay at the back of where the garage had been.

"Take it easy, Rash. And Michael…"

Michael was ten yards away and gaining speed with every stride. He would run to the hospital. He should have gone there first thing. The big man… probably the red Sierra… dented front door… could be there now.

No one gave chase. Araf was no longer bothering with small fry. J J walked over to Rashid, put her hand on his arm, and in a feigned tone of shock said, "Your hair needs combing."

Rashid automatically brought his hands up to his head but stopped himself from running them through his hair. That's what she wanted him to do. Everything was always on her terms. At times he felt like a puppet.

"So what? It's not every day that one's family business is bombed into extinction."

"You haven't done those photographs either, have you?"

He turned away wishing she wasn't there complicating matters, confusing him, making him even more nervous than he usually was when Araf was around. Araf swaggered and twitched up to him. He carried a short length of lead piping, symbol of the new resolve, with which he kept rapping the palm of his free hand.

"Your Dad's place this, innit?"

Rashid nodded.

"Time we sorted them, Rashid."

J J's chin dropped in mock admiration, "Wow! Araf the Enforcer brings peace back to the troubled streets of Brancaster!"

Araf pointed the piping towards J J but kept facing Rashid. "You keep out of this!"

"Don't talk stupid then! Let the police sort it out."

Rashid did comb his hair with his hands now, out of nervousness. Araf turned slowly towards J J.

"Police probably 'elp them. Now, get lost. You don't belong 'ere or 'adn't you noticed the colour of your skin." There was no response from the gang members to Araf's joke. He looked around. Imran laughed, "Nice one," and the others followed suit.

Rashid spoke, "Leave her alone. She's OK."

J J raised her arms wide as if in celebration and spoke directly to Imran.

"Hey, Rashid thinks I'm O.K. Life now has meaning."

Imran smiled shyly. Rashid winced. Araf ignored her

and surveyed the mess around them.

"You with us?"

Rashid wished JJ was a thousand miles away. He nodded sheepishly. Araf bent his head closer and pretended to clean out an ear with his finger.

"Sorry, didn't 'ear that, Rashid."

Rashid's answer was an angry shout: "Yes! Yes! OK?"

Araf tapped him on the shoulder with the piping. "Pleased to 'ear it."

"And I don't believe I'm hearing it." Rashid saw the change. JJ had been trying to keep it jokey, use her humour to defuse what was happening, make them see how ridiculous they looked and sounded. She had stopped that now and was angry. "He's as bad as the idiots who burnt the garage, Rashid."

Araf had started to walk on with the others following, but hearing JJ, spun round quickly and half-raised the lead piping. For a split-second, Rashid thought they were going to get a demonstration of the crazy, headstrong Araf and his capacity for mindless violence. Araf stared hard at JJ, breathing noisily. JJ stood her ground and started to smile. It was all so ridiculous. Araf stepped towards her but stopped. This was a girl. He opted for cool, for control. He tilted his head, chewed and leered at JJ.

"You should forget about 'er," he said to Rashid. He looked JJ up and down. "Shouldn't be 'ard."

JJ put her hands on her hips and stuck her tongue out. Araf turned, raised an arm in the air and indicated that his cavalry was moving out. As he passed Rashid, he spat out, "This afternoon. Simpson's Mill. A little ceremony."

Ellen Hassan did not go to her sister's but to her brother-

81

in-law's Finance and Property Consultancy. Tahir's office was sparsely furnished: a long desk and three chairs all with tubular steel legs and frames; a coat-stand in the same style; a tall, empty, black bookcase, and, on the wall, a modern painting made up of squares, rectangles and triangles. Tahir's business was doing well; according to a special feature in the Brancaster Times, it was "a success story written by a rising star in the local political firmament."

Their talk was punctuated regularly by the ringing of telephones in the outer-office. Tahir's secretary dealt with them. He had told her that, on no account was his meeting with Ellen to be interrupted. "Not even if it's the Bank of England," he joked.

Tahir stayed behind his paper-free desk. Ellen looked directly at him, a boldness he disliked intensely. Tahir was unlike his brother in looks, short and portly while Farouk was of above-average height and slim. Farouk had a full head of hair, but although Tahir's hair was thick and straggly at the sides, the dome of his head was bald. Once the door was closed he told Ellen not to beat about the bush. She must have a very special reason for swallowing her pride and coming to see him and he had an idea what it was. Ellen told him that she and Farouk were in serious financial trouble. "She and Farouk": Tahir didn't like this idea of shared financial responsibility at all. What was wrong with his brother? The man should hold those reins.

"This is very hard for me, Ellen, and whatever you do, you must not take this personally."

"You've never liked me."

Tahir placed both hands on the desert desktop and

spread his fingers wide. "Liking doesn't come into it. We were hurt deeply when Farouk married you. You must understand, our community has beliefs, traditions which must be preserved…"

"We were in love."

"When someone ignores such things, he threatens the existence of our community…"

"We are in love."

"… the… the purity of our culture."

Ellen was beginning to wish she hadn't come. The visit was bringing back unpleasant memories of hard words spoken and tears shed before she and Farouk had married. "A loan; that's all, to tide us over."

"We… as a people, have to stay together."

Ellen got up to leave, "You won't help."

Tahir remained seated and gestured with his palms upwards, "I'd like to, but… Farouk should come himself. He should not have sent you."

Ellen was at the door, "He didn't."

★ ★ ★ ★ ★

Avril was very nice in more ways than one, thought Bob Brady; late-thirties, accent from down south somewhere, a good-looker with a bubbly personality and a sense of humour. "We're just one, big, happy family, but don't you suggest for one minute that I'm old enough to be the mother of anyone here!" As manager of Turner's Garage, she had given him a quick tour of the building: the large service area, delivery bay, stores, another large bay and workshop that was, "Well, privately run, really, Bob, and out of bounds, OK?" And finally, Reception – "Basically, your little kingdom, Bob. Front man, first one a customer sees, so it's very important you make them happy. Any problems, technical questions or otherwise, have a word with the others. Jake'll fill you in on the details of the job as such. Welcome aboard. Ciao."

The morning had been fairly busy: a few telephone calls, a couple of saloon cars for servicing that Bob had checked in and driven into the service area, a delivery of electrical components, a few smiles from Avril as she went through reception, the quick crossword in *The Sun* and some cleaning and coffee-making. It wasn't what he was used to and it wasn't what he called a real job, but it was a job and he was glad to have it.

The mechanics asked him to join them in the local during the lunch hour, but Bob turned them down. On his first day, he wanted to stay close to the job, make himself more familiar with everything. The hour, and then another passed and no one returned. Apart from the petrol pump attendant who stuck close to his small kiosk, Bob seemed to be the only person left on the premises. He checked the appointments schedule: three bookings but they had all been cancelled. Avril's initials were alongside. Eating one of the sausage, fried egg and brown sauce sandwiches he had made himself that morning, Bob wandered about the garage interior. In the service area, tools had been abandoned on the floor in the middle of jobs; Radio 1 was playing on a transistor. He stuck his head into side rooms; a workshop; the paint store. He felt good. As the only one left, he was in charge. This was something he had missed during the last fifteen months; the responsibilities a job brought with it.

He had been curious, as anyone would be, when Avril

had referred to the privately run, *out of bounds* section of the garage. The service area was L-shaped, with the smaller part occupied by two old yellow Escorts a mechanic was working on in his spare time. The inside entry to the private loading bay was at the corner of the L. Bob shoved the last large portion of sandwich into his mouth as he reached the door, catching a glimpse as he did so of blue mould on a stubby finger of sausage that stuck out between the bread slices. How long had the sausage been in the fridge? Two weeks? Should be all right. It's penicillin anyway, isn't it?

The padlock was unfastened. Bob thought there would be no harm in having a look. The large overhead outer door to the bay was closed but the interior was well-lit by skylights and powerful lamps. A workbench ran almost the length of one side, and a full range of mechanics' tools were fastened to the wall above. A van that had been resprayed and still had masking tape and protective paper attached stood at the centre of the floor space over a boarded inspection pit. Bob noticed that the back number plate was half-off and that a replacement with a new registration lay on the floor nearby.

"Avril say you could come in 'ere?"

It was said quietly but it still made him jump. Jake Gillery had heard him entering and had hidden behind the door. He put an arm around Bob's shoulder.

"No, not really. I were curious."

"Killed the cat that, didn't it?"

Bob made an attempt to laugh. He couldn't gauge Jake's mood. He was speaking slowly, separating the words, as if Bob was deaf.

"We believe in doing what we're told 'ere, Bob."

"Fair enough. Me too."

"This is a special room for special work. Get me drift?"

"Political like – Group 88?"

"Work we keep very quiet about. And I'm not talking about just giving a Paki a good kickin'."

"No problem."

Jake's face allowed itself a smile, "No 'arm, I suppose. You're one of us really." He patted Bob on the back and returned to removing the registration plate. Bob stepped further into the bay.

"Avril's a bit cautious like. She'll want to get to know you better before she trusts you. Then you'll get some of our... em... special work."

"No problem, Jake. Where is everyone?"

"Bit of a flap on. Big meeting tonight and... em... some of that special work. An end-job, you might say."

"End-job?"

Jake looked up at Bob grinning broadly, "A car like, yeh, old car ready for t'scrapyard but still on t'road, moor road. We've got to get it off. OK?"

Bob grinned back at him, "Foreign make like?"

Jake laughed, "Too bloody true."

Bob held his grin. *The moor road... the old man with the accent... beaten, Michael had said... nearly dead... an end-job on an old foreign car.*

Jake was still laughing. "You'll do all right 'ere, Bob. You're OK."

Chapter 9

They all went from Araf's "office", stepping through more filing cabinet confetti,

a woven fabric is made up of two elements – the warp, or longitudinal threads; and the weft, or cross threads,

into what had been the carding room of Simpson's Mill. Nothing in the structure now resembled the long, high-ceilinged room that had been there. Because the interior had been in a dangerous condition, all the internal ceilings and walls had been demolished leaving a huge cavern spanned by massive girders. Wide stone stairs still clung to the end of the building and Araf led the way up these to what had been the third and the highest floor. Three of them, Rashid, Imran and Araf stood on the landing, a broad slab, while the others remained on the stairs.

"That ceremony I were tellin' you about. Your initiation."

Araf pointed to large stones, spaced about a metre apart, that jutted inward from the wall between the girders. Before Araf spoke again, Rashid realised what they wanted him to do. To prove himself he had to get to the first girder and then walk the breadth of the mill along it. Imran was uneasy; he started to say something to Araf, but stopped. The others were quiet, frightened and excited.

As always, Rashid had showered that morning and had used an expensive deodorant, but the smell that filled his nostrils then was his own sweat which was patchily soaking his shirt. He started to take his leather jacket off, but stopped. He didn't want them to see just how nervous he was. Imran gestured that he would hold it, but Rashid shook his head.

"Walk – no crawling. OK?"

Rashid told himself not to delay. If he hesitated, he would have doubts about doing it; he would get more nervous; they would start to taunt him, call him a coward, call him a nowt.

"After this, you're norra nowt any more. You're one of us."

"No problem."

Rashid looked down once before he started – a mistake – his knees quivered and his bowels loosened as if he was going to… going to… No, please; not that. He took a deep breath and levelled his gaze across the great mill interior. The sun plunged through a high unboarded window and its ray, crowded with motes, bisected Rashid's gaze and struck the far wall. "Stone-dust and perhaps flecks of wool from years ago," thought Rashid. He flattened himself against the wall, put one foot on to the first jutting stone, tested it to see that it would take his weight, and then brought his other foot there. Just enough room. Don't pause too long. Don't look down. One more stone, then the girder. One foot; the other; the second stone. Right foot to the girder, then the left. Made it. Without thinking, he went down on all fours.

"On your feet, Nowt. 'Ard bit now."

Rashid looked back to the landing. Imran was saying something quietly to Araf. Rashid saw Araf sneer and push him away. He wondered if the mighty Araf had ever walked the girder. If he, Rashid, was going to do it, it would have to be done now and quickly. Don't look down. Scenes from a dozen or more videos rushed into his mind: dizzying cliff-face struggles; film stars tumbling into black abysses; a silent movie comedian bumbling along the edge of a precipice; circus acts gone wrong; heroes in free-fall over a kaleidoscope of fields, forests and villages. Rashid stood upright. The girder was a good half-a-metre wide but looked like a tightrope. He breathed deeply, put his arms out from his side for balance, and started to walk.

"We'll gerra couple of bin liners to tek you 'ome in!" Araf shouted, but was told to keep quiet by an angry Imran. Araf tensed, looked hard at his right-hand man, thought about disciplining him, but then shrugged his shoulders and turned back to enjoy the entertainment.

Almost level with his eyes and directly above where the girder penetrated the wall opposite, Rashid saw a hole in the stone where an overflow pipe had been. Starlings used it year after year to build their nests and Rashid saw the sharp, decisive movements of feeding going on and then the sudden inflow of light, shutter open, as the parent-bird left. For a moment, he wondered who the people in the van at the farmhouse were and if they *had* wanted to kill the old man, and if it was one of them that Michael had disturbed in the hospital. He should have enlarged the photographs for J J.

In his mind's eye, he drew a lifeline from the starlings' hole to his body. Taking alternate glances at his feet and at the nesting place, Rashid "pulled" himself forward slowly along this line.

"You don't 'ave t'do this, Rashid." It was Imran. Bit late now. Rashid kept going and didn't turn his head. He heard some shouts and scuffling on the landing. He was doing well and gaining in confidence. He was going to make it.

"Braindead! Get off there!"

Not the landing. Down below. J J. Don't look!

Rashid looked. J J ran through the scattered papers to be almost directly below him.

"Stay still!"

Easier said than done. Rashid wobbled. The girder was moving like a tightrope; swinging. Ridiculous! Rashid kept looking down. Mustn't fall on J J. He looked up, level, heard the chicks clamouring for food, heard a faint flutter of wings as a parent returned; shutter closed. Those people in the van could be killers. Rashid slipped, one leg went over the side of the girder, the other crumpled under him. Should have changed into the old jeans. What did she have to come for? Sticking her nose in; white girl organising everyone. For one very short moment, the idea of falling felt good. It would get him off this stupid girder and away from stupid Araf with his stupid ideas. And he'd get a bit of sympathy and maybe even affection from J J. Fat chance. In his half-kneeling position, Rashid clung to the girder and didn't think he would be able to move forward or back ever.

"Don't move!"

The gang charged down the stone stairs making rhythmic grunting noises. Araf shouted to Rashid.

"Too bad! You failed! You're still a nowt!"

When they had gone, J J stood for a moment looking upwards at the paralysed Rashid.

"Your hair's a mess."

This brought Rashid out of his numbness. He went to

brush his hair back, wobbled once more and had to fall forward and hug the girder to secure himself. The red band slipped from his head and fell to the floor. Down below, J J shook her head in bewilderment.

"Don't move a muscle!"

She ran like Rashid had never seen her do before, up the stairs to the top landing. There, she began to speak to him like she had never done before, softly, affectionately, but not with too much emotion because that wouldn't help Rashid in his predicament. Gradually, J J persuaded Rashid to turn around and crawl slowly back to the wall and step along the embedded stones. She hugged him fiercely when he got to her.

Outside, J J walked very fast keeping her hands in the pockets of her ragged woollen jacket all the time as if she was frightened what she might do with them if she took them out. Every so often, she would stop, flap her arms like a crow with feathers missing and shout at Rashid.

"You could have killed yourself, braindead." The softness, the obvious affection, had gone from her speech.

"I never knew you cared."

"Course I care! I want you to have my babies, remember."

"Always a joke."

"Not true. Nearly always."

Rashid walked on. He wanted to enlarge the photographs. Halfway through Araf's dangerous initiation ceremony, an understanding had come to him. It was stupid, wrong to try to compromise with bullies like Araf. They had to be confronted. Leo Meyer had been bullied.

J J called from a few yards behind, "Playing soldiers."

"Araf's not playing any more. It's serious. Street patrols,

everything."

"Seriously stupid."

"You don't understand."

J J caught him up and took his hand just as they reached the top of his terrace. As usual, her timing was right off and Rashid tried to disentangle his fingers from hers.

"Did you think of me when you were on that girder?"

Rashid didn't reply.

"I bet you thought, 'If I fall, I'll never be consumed by her passion; I'll never know the soft, loving warmth of her body next to mine.'"

Rashid got his hand free. His father had pulled up outside the house and was going in the front door. Respect women. He was trying to. He wished J J would show him more respect and more sensitivity about how to behave when his parents were about.

It was not a happy house and it was obvious to the young people when they entered that they had interrupted an argument. Ellen Hassan's small, anxious features quickly put on a forced smile and she was friendlier than ever towards J J, asking after her family, progress in school, plans for the summer holiday, anything to distract them and herself from the upset of Farouk's reaction to her visiting Tahir.

Rashid was glad to get into the dark room. As J J watched, he worked silently, making enlargements of the negatives she had indicated. He concentrated hard, determined to do a good job. As the first images started to form in the developing fluid, Rashid began once again to question what had happened to Leo Meyer: he told himself it was silly, that there was no real evidence, but there was something about the way one of the men was jumping out of the van that convinced him. It reminded Rashid of soldiers jumping from Land Rovers in Northern Ireland. His right foot had just touched the ground, the other was still in the air and his whole body looked tense, ready for action, for a fight, perhaps to kill.

"Why should someone want to kill him?" he asked J J.

"It's something to do with the war, with the concentration camps."

Rashid put the print through his stop bath and into the fixer. "You said there was no tattoo."

"He is Jewish. Michael said they put it on the forms at the hospital."

"Could be a disguise – I mean, a good cover. Perhaps he's pretending he's Jewish because he's got something to hide."

"Like a war criminal, you mean? Something to do with that trial that's on the news."

"Maybe."

Before Rashid washed and dried the prints, they studied them closely. Rashid had done well. The three men and the woman could be identified easily from the sequence of shots.

Chapter 10

Julia Brady should have been used to working nights, she'd done it so many times over the years, but her body-clock never accepted this argument. She never had the same quality of sleep as she did when she worked days, and was always very slow to come round. Usually, she would stay in her dressing gown, drink coffee, feed herself, smoke one or two cigarettes (Simon Leighton had suggested hypnosis to stop this habit), do a little housework and try to avoid Bob Brady. The free hours would disappear quickly with perhaps, one or two of them – never enough – spent with Simon when he finished work at about six.

It was quarter to five. Julia was still in her dressing gown, still feeling very ragged and tired, when the flat began to fill up with people.

Bob was the first to arrive and sulked when Julia didn't ask right away how the day at the garage had gone. When she did ask, "Great, fine, no problem," was his brief reply and then he retreated to the small kitchen to fry his supper.

About ten minutes after Bob, Julia was very surprised to find Simon ringing the doorbell and Michael with him. She was surprised and flustered, and her voice, in Simon's presence, became giggly, almost silly. Simon should have rung, then Julia would have dressed and straightened herself out. Simon told her not to worry about that; it wasn't a social call. There was an edge to his voice that worried Julia. Michael, as usual, looked down at the floor and drew the curtains across his face.

No, Simon assured Julia, he wasn't angry. No profit in

anger. Confused matters. However, it had to stop. He had specifically asked Michael not to hang around the hospital; had told him categorically that the old man was in safe hands, and had, in no uncertain terms, stated that, in his opinion, Leo Meyer was not being hunted and that Michael was letting his imagination run away with his sense.

Julia felt awful about what had happened. She couldn't stop apologising. She tried to love her son, but at times like this, she wished that he and his father were a million miles away and she had a life on her own, or, as she was hoping more and more, with Simon. He was good for her, and it wasn't simply his money and lifestyle that she found attractive. He was caring and thoughtful. He seldom came round without bringing her a little gift of flowers or chocolates. Julia felt younger when she was with him, felt reprieved from the drab, early-ageing process that her marriage to Bob had become.

"Hiding in Mr Meyer's bathroom. Staff Nurse Trimble found him."

Michael started to say something about guarding Leo but his mother cut him off by apologising once more to Simon. He decided that his best policy, as usual, was to stay silent, and, as usual, to run when he got the opportunity.

Bob Brady came into the living room singing and carrying a plate of bacon, sausage and eggs. He was out of the sulks, out of tune, feeling good again after his day's work and looking forward to supper in front of the telly. The last people he wanted to see were Michael looking as if he'd just had a telling off and The Suit, Lover-Boy, the man he had lost his wife to. He stopped singing abruptly.

"... *for me Argentina. The truth is I never...* What's up wi' 'im?"

Simon started to explain, "Michael's been trying to help an old man he thinks was attacked."

Bob put his plate on the table and stepped back to face Simon, "I'm norr asking you."

"Simon's trying to help . Don't be so childish."

Michael saw his father's neck muscles bunch and his lower jaw set hard as he clenched his teeth in anger. In the tight knot of his angry mind, Bob Brady was on the late night streets again and effing and blinding and kicking, and the bundle on the ground, moaning softly wasn't a Paki, but Lover-Boy.

Michael had to get out of the flat and back to the hospital. Leo Meyer was in danger.

The bell rang and Michael's mother opened the door to J J and Rashid.

"A house-full," Julia said, laughed nervously, and then slipped into her bedroom to get dressed. The two adults remaining stood awkwardly at either end of the settee.

"Michael's not doing anyone any good by hanging round the hospital," said Simon calmly.

Bob Brady saw Rashid over Simon's shoulder: Suits and Foreigners; they're taking over, even in his own home. "It's norr a crime."

"No, but a nuisance. We can't allow it, I'm afraid." Simon pulled a suit sleeve back and looked at his watch. He had a meeting to attend.

J J was another one who hadn't any time to waste. She waved the pack of enlargements at Michael. "We've got photos of the ones who beat him up."

After that announcement, she acted as if the adults

weren't there. Her voice was urgent. There were things to be done. She went to the table and the other two followed. Once Michael had seen the photographs, they had to go to Leo Meyer once more and then to the police. Rashid was very quiet. He felt Bob Brady's unspoken resentment, as bad as the girder-walk in its own way. J J pushed Bob's supper plate from its place and spread the prints on the table.

"He doesn't want us to go to the police," said Michael.

"Well, too bad. We're going. It's for his own good."

"Are any of this lot the one you saw at the hospital, Michael?"

Michael looked hard and shook his head: "Not big enough. 'E were tall and… awkward. You know what I mean? 'Eavy. Shambly. Darker hair."

Michael looked for more anger from his father. He expected him to tell them to get the photographs off the table and to clear out. He was surprised when he found his father standing right behind him looking at the photographs with interest. His supper was congealing fast but he took and studied several of the prints.

J J quipped, "Friends of yours?" and Michael who had learned to understand his father's facial expressions and temper as some people read the weather, now saw a look that had never shown itself before. Behind the eyes, alongside the fury, there was a hint of fear. It went as quickly as it had come. Bob Brady's complexion whitened and he stared blankly back at J J.

"What's so special about this old guy, anyway?"

"We think he's Jewish. Something to do with the concentration camps in the war."

"Years ago that," he answered dully. "All exaggerated

anyway."

JJ looked at Rashid and Michael in turn, a look which said she didn't really believe this conversation was taking place.

"Five and not six million Jews killed. That what you mean?"

The weather-map of his father's face was easier for Michael to read now. Bob Brady was furious. He didn't have to take this in his own home from a… from a… girl… some posh girl. Simon Leighton saw the warning signs as well and stepped across to the table. He picked up one of the photographs.

"Perhaps you should respect Mr Meyer's wishes and not involve the police. It could be some family feud. You'd be surprised what goes on."

Bob Brady sat down at the table, pushed the prints away from his place and sawed with his knife at a strip of very streaky bacon. "Perhaps you should just stop messin' in things you don't understand before you get 'urt!"

Simon gave the young people a "smile-and-raised-eyebrows look" which was intended to tell them that adult pride was hurt but don't worry, one adult present did understand them. He steered the conversation on to less difficult ground.

"They're good photos."

"Rash… Rashid has his own darkroom at home, all the equipment."

"Well done."

Michael heard the familiar clacking of his father's teeth on metal as he took food from the fork. He was eating more quickly than usual and seemed very agitated. Although his mouth was full, he had to speak, "Used to be *the* residential area round here where 'e lives."

And J J had to retort, "It's still a very nice area."

"Nice? They 'ang washin' in t' front gardens!"

Julia walked in from the bedroom, with a smile pinned anxiously on her face and behind the smile a wish that the young ones would go out of the house and Bob out of her life. She crossed the room to be at Simon's side. Perhaps they could eat out somewhere before she started work.

Bob Brady, feeling a stranger in his own home and in his own country, pushed his cold, unappetising meal away from him, stood up and said that he had to get out. Rashid stepped quickly to one side to let him past.

Julia Brady gave a nervous, schoolgirl giggle. Simon said he had to get to a meeting. "Awkward time but I couldn't reschedule it." Julia said she'd come with him anyway.

J J, Michael and Rashid had the place to themselves and an hour to wait until visiting time at the hospital. Michael couldn't stay still. He was sure Leo Meyer was in danger and that they should be with him. J J told him to calm down but Michael was anxious, needed to do something. He said he would cook for them but J J stopped him. She had been put off eating anything at the Brady's by the sight of Michael's father stuffing himself with cold dead pig. She let him get them some orange juice.

She then told Michael to switch on the television for the six o'clock news. Rashid was about to tell her to stop giving orders when J J said that they had to make some decisions: Michael and she would go to the hospital to check on Leo; Rashid would call at his home for the negatives and then come to the hospital. The police would want to see the negatives as well as the prints and even if the old man tried to stop them, they were going to involve the police.

Michael nodded. Rashid started to say that he was thrilled to be part of the decision-making process, but J J told him to shut up there was something on the telly about the war crimes trial:

> *… how the high-ranking Scheffler could have remained at a distance from the prisoners and the gassings. However, he chose, frequently, to join in the routine vicious treatment meted out to the camp inmates. Mr. Goldfarb, a survivor of Auschwitz, related how, after rumours of an escape, Scheffler had personally whipped a prisoner and that the man had died from his wounds.*

A still of the accused came on to the screen, the same photograph J J had seen on television two nights earlier and on the newspaper cutting at the farmhouse: big ears, shaven head, that haunted look, the face Leo Meyer had put a cross through. What had Leo Meyer to do with this man and with Auschwitz?

Chapter 11

Rashid didn't think twice about the white Ford Transit van outside his house. He didn't bother looking at the driver or the woman in the passenger seat and didn't notice that the engine was running. Just behind a parade of shops, theirs was a popular street for parking on.

The foot of the front door always stuck against the jamb. He kicked hard to free it. Inside, there was no answer when he called and Rashid remembered that, to smooth things over and cheer them both up, Ellen had persuaded Farouk to go to a restaurant that evening.

Rashid always closed the darkroom door and always insisted that his parents did the same if they went in there. When he saw that it was open, he was annoyed. Like his bedroom, it was his space which he respected and kept tidy and which he wanted others to respect.

Rashid tried to open the door further but it jammed against equipment littering the floor inside. His darkroom had been ransacked: drawers had been pulled out and emptied on to the floor; trays, bottles and papers had been scattered. His enlarger lay on its side.

Rashid's mind didn't want to understand what this meant. He backed away from the door. He had to get someone: J J.

They had been very quiet. Two of them; perhaps three, it was hard to tell. Rashid never heard a sound. The arm swung like a scythe-blade into his stomach and he doubled over in pain. He was grabbed, hit, knocked one way then the other. He closed and opened his eyes. Odd bits of his attackers: a hand, (black leather gloves); foot (trekking boots, black, size 8, perhaps 9); a back (sweatshirt, royal blue); a leg (loosefit jeans, blue-black), and odd bits of the room: his mother's *Best of Bread* album, the tapestry of the Ka'ba above the sideboard; a pile of freshly ironed clothes on a dining chair all flashed jerkily in front of him like frames in a badly spliced cine-film.

They didn't speak. Not a word. Rashid screamed that there was no money in the house. They held him still and tight, pressed up against the wall. One of them went through his pockets and took the prints. Another, maybe two, turned over the living room, pulling out drawers, scattering ornaments, going through his father's box files of accounts.

Rashid slumped to the floor when they left: the white van outside, a Ford Transit; the same Ford Transit? The same people? After a few minutes, he got up again and stumbled to the darkroom. He knew without looking what else they had taken but had to check. He was right. Every single one of the albums where he stored his negatives had been stolen.

Half an hour later, J J and Michael reached Leo Meyer's room in the intensive care unit of Brancaster General. Leo Meyer was not there.

It was J J who had the idea. Michael would never have thought of it. It seemed so pointless. Michael couldn't have thought of it because Leo Meyer's disappearance was another of his failures and a dark storm had risen and filled his mind with memories of other failures and his parents' comments: *you can do much better than this; no real staying power; always take the easy way; let people walk over you; give up far too easily; you're lazy.* Run; search the hospital corridors for the "shambly" man in the heavy dark blue trousers and the car parks for the red, battered Sierra. That was all Michael could think of doing. It was J J who said that they should check at Reception.

"Yes, Mr Meyer has left... Forty minutes ago, maybe... No, he was not picked up. Mr Meyer discharged himself against the wishes of the hospital authorities. And if anyone wants my opinion – not that they would in this place – he's a foolish old man."

They left a note for Rashid and went in search of Leo. He would head for his home, J J was certain, and to do that he needed a taxi or a bus. The taxi ranks were right outside the hospital and the bus station was within easy walking distance.

The taxis were shunting quickly to new positions in the busy rank. J J and Michael walked alongside asking the drivers if they had seen Leo. They shrugged and shook their heads or didn't listen. Michael irritated J J by pulling at her sleeve and saying over and over that they had to find him.

The town centre was busy: in an attempt to stimulate business, many of the shops were still open and, in the Cathedral Gardens, a rock group was about to start the first of a series of summer concerts sponsored by the Brancaster Chamber of Commerce. Michael went ahead of J J to the bus station, running through the pedestrian precinct with its dried-up fountain, weaving in and out of the shoppers, sometimes having to stop, wait until he saw a gap, skip through it and run once more, all the time telling himself that he hadn't failed, that he had been given another opportunity, that *they*, whoever they were, hadn't got Leo Meyer. J J half-ran, half-walked and tried to think what she and Michael were going to do if they found the old man. He might just tell them to clear off, leave him alone, as he had done at the farmhouse.

Ahead of her and surrounded by shoppers who had rested their loads, was a casually-dressed young man carrying an expensive portable tape-recorder. Radio Brancaster had sent a reporter on to the streets to record a *vox pop* on the Deliverance Party's policy of separate development.

J J slowed down as she got nearer. The small crowd was an even mix of Asians and whites and their responses were positive: *Well, different races have their own ways, haven't they?… Nothin' against them like, but you just get on better, on the whole, with your own… That Gilmore talks a lot of sense… This society will always regard us as second class unless we are allowed to develop on our own… It's like survival, really… see which survives… evolution and all that.*

J J saw Michael turning right at the end of the precinct. The short hill that was Townson Street would take him to the station. She had to stop and have her say. She pushed through the people, grabbed the microphone from the startled reporter and told him, the crowd and anyone who would listen to the broadcast that evening that people were people no matter what colour their skin was or what their religion was or where they were from and they ought to be able to get on together and if they didn't, and if they listened to the stupid Deliverance Party, we could all go back to what happened in Europe with the Jews and all the others, and it just showed that we were stupid and hadn't learned a thing. She heard comments from all around her, "Just a kid", "What does she know about the war?", "Nothin' to do wi' Jews."

Rashid had given a statement to the police as quickly as he could and sneaked out, leaving them with a very upset Farouk and Ellen Hassan. He was carrying bad news, but when he heard J J's voice from fifty metres away and when she emerged, flushed and angry, from the crowd, he gave her a big smile and a hug. She pushed him off.

"I didn't say what I really wanted to say and I lost the thread at the end. And what do I have to shout for? It was useless."

"It was brilliant. I couldn't have done it."

As they headed towards the bus station, J J was still going over in her head what she should have said and not listening properly to what Rashid was telling her.

"They took the prints and the negatives. That's what they were after. We've nothing for the police."

J J stopped, asked him to repeat what he had said and when he did, she put the interlude with the reporter behind her. "How did they know about the photographs?"

"I've been trying to work that one out. No idea, unless they saw us on the moor. And that man in the red car found out where I live."

They turned on to Townson Street and started climbing up the hill. They were half-way to the bus station before J J spoke again. When she spoke, it was hesitantly. She was reluctant to say what she did.

"Michael's dad knew about the photos."

Michael was sitting, slumped forward, beside Leo Meyer in the queue for the second of the two, daily 632 service buses, the only ones to travel the Brereton Moor road. No one else was waiting there. The old man sat very upright and still, as if frightened of spilling what little strength he had through unnecessary movement. He didn't turn when J J spoke to him. He was going home, he told her. The fox had to be fed. They must not interfere. He was ready to accept whatever happened. No, he wouldn't go to the police; he didn't like people in uniforms.

"Someone *is* trying to kill you, aren't they?"

Leo tapped his hands on his knees but said nothing.

"They're bound to go back to the farmhouse."

"What happens, happens. I've lived long enough."

"Why do they want to kill you?"

"You want to know? You really want to know?"

Leo looked at each of the young people in turn, children who were jostling their way into his life, trying to tell him what to do. What did they know about anything, their lives all American films and food from packets? Why should he even speak to them? The dark boy, the Asian, the one so fussy about his clothes, seemed to read his thoughts.

"It's wrong to let bullies push you around."

Bullies: his life had been full of bullies; his every dream was crowded with bullies. What could this child tell him, Leo Meyer, about bullies? And then, his heart thumping, bigger than his chest, Leo Meyer was back there again, the place he could never erase from his memory, the evil land of giant bullies, and Uncle Eliahu, always clumsy, like a clown stumbling or pretending to, was falling in the mud and splashing that man's boots, HIS immaculate boots, the boots young Leo cleaned, and he he, HE, HE, HE, HE!!! THAT MAN! was raising his pistol and the fury that was his alone erupted in his face, the face young Leo shaved, and HE was hitting gentle, dark Uncle

Eliahu, the one who could conjure eggs from behind his ears – bloodied now – and blow coins from his nose; hitting, hitting, hitting and Uncle Eliahu was falling again and HE was aiming his gun. And HE fired. And HE was smiling.

"They should be punished," said Rashid.

Out of the mouth of babes and sucklings hast Thou ordained strength. The words of these children were so true, so uncomplicatedly true that Leo Meyer wanted to scream from the ache they brought to his conscience. He had to get away from these children. Shakily, he got to his feet.

"These people want to finish the job they started at Auschwitz in 1942." Leo stared straight at Michael and thought how the boy's long hair would have been reason enough for them to kill him. Breathlessly, with strange whimpering sounds between his words, he asked them, "Auschwitz: what's Auschwitz to you?"

J J knew she was right. It was that trial. Rashid said, "But you haven't got a tattoo." Leo started to reply but his body folded like a paper lantern.

Michael and J J knelt to help the still-conscious Leo, but Rashid's attention was caught by the sight of a vehicle nudging its snub nose around the corner of the bus company office at the far end of the station. Michael and J J couldn't understand why he was so excited.

"There was a white Transit outside my house. It's the one in the photos, I'm sure. It's had a respray!"

"We've got to take him somewhere safe."

J J looked around the abandoned office, bare except for one large desk. "You're sure he'll be safe here?"

Michael nodded: "I'm stoppin'. I'll mek sure 'e is."

"And make sure your Dad doesn't find out."

"It wasn't 'im. Dad's stupid but not that stupid."

Michael flicked the hair from the front of his face. J J was looking right at him. She was angry.

"I think we should drop it," said Rashid from the window. "The damage has been done."

Rashid was nervous. Taking care not to be seen, he looked from one side of the window, over the sign, GILMORE PROPERTY SERVICES, down on to the quiet city centre. A tramp was rummaging through a waste bin outside the McDonald's on York Street. Rashid saw he was wearing battered Reebok pump trainers. He spoke without turning to the others.

"We can't keep him here for long. And we need some more evidence before we can go to the police."

J J bent down to Leo who was wrapped in Michael's sleeping bag and sitting up against the desk. "It would help if you told us more. Nothing makes sense until you do."

Leo's head ached. Her words came to him as if he was receiving a telephone call from a distant land on a poor line, "Beat the bullies, eh?"

"He can't hear you properly," said Rashid.

J J raised her voice: "Why are they trying to kill you? It's fifty years after the war."

Children; they were not much more than children. They were already in danger and if he told them more, that danger would increase. But children have consciences; fourteen-year-old Leo Meyer had known right from wrong, hadn't he? And had done nothing. But what could I do, a child? Something. Something. The razor at Scheffler's throat. Something... I could

110

have done something!

"Is it to do with the trial? That man Bauer?" said J J.

Leo heard that clearly and shocked her by sniggering.

"That one was a *grüne spitze*, a common criminal with special duties. He hit prisoners, kicked them, but it was nothing."

"Nothing!"

"Kisses, believe me. He is not the man they think he is. That one is still free."

J J pressed him for more information and as she did so, she felt Rashid getting agitated. He wanted her to let the old man rest, to stop always pushing to get things done, to have all the answers.

"How do you know this Bauer isn't the right one?"

Leo did not answer immediately. He rubbed at his eyes as if they were strained and then spoke.

"For a while, I was a servant to Scheffler: cleaning his room, polishing his boots. I even shaved him."

"If you saw him, you'd know him?"

"Only his wife knew him better."

"And that's why these people in the van are after you?"

Leo nodded, "Possibly. Nazis, new and old."

"Then why don't you say? Tell the police."

Rashid had to speak, "Leave him alone, J J. Don't bully him. Let him make his own decisions."

Making decisions: acting on those decisions. Leo's face took on a pained expression and he was once more in Auschwitz where Miriam and others were being herded by Scheffler with his whip, into Bunker 1, the gas chamber her own father had helped build. His memory painted her with beautiful hair, thick, raven-coloured and

111

hanging almost to her waist, hair they had cut and shaved when the family arrived at the camp. Why had he let them do those things to his gentle sister?

Leo shook his head at J J. "So many died. I did nothing."

* * * * *

"What dragon would St. George set out to slay were he alive and living in Britain today? What fair maiden would he rescue? Here in Brancaster, we have a developing situation…"

The small hall was two-thirds full. A picket-fence of burly young men in black trousers and black T-shirts stood facing the audience with their backs to the three-sided stage. Two were mechanics from Turner's Garage. Hedley Gilmore strode about behind them as he delivered his speech, the stage cleared, as he always insisted, of anything he might be tempted to lean on. His hands were free of papers, for Hedley Gilmore never spoke from notes. If one believed in something as deeply as he did, one didn't need prompts. And people appreciated that. No notes and no hesitation. Truth wasn't a stammerer.

"In no way can I be labelled a racist. A common-sensist, that's what I am, and common-sense tells me that separate development for different races is the only way to proceed. Experience tells me the same. The recent, deplorable attacks underline the simple, common-sense fact that there are huge gaps between the races which can never be bridged. In no way do I condone such attacks and I wish to place it on public record now, that my party and I personally are in no way connected with such goings on. We believe wholeheartedly in British democracy and the democratic process. However, let no one conclude that we in the Deliverance Party of Great Britain are pusillanimous. If violence is offered to my party workers, then rest assured, they will defend themselves, and do so with great effect."

Someone shouted from the audience. The picket fence shifted slightly, but the troublemaker was dealt with by Jake Gillery who was sitting at the back of the hall with Bob Brady. He dragged the heckler from his seat and pushed him out of an exit. The incident hardly interrupted Hedley Gilmore's flow.

"Repatriation has been made a dirty word by some. Let's look – in a common-sense way – at what we really mean by that word. Repatriation…"

Afterwards, Bob suggested they go to The Lion but Jake shook his head.

"No drink. Big job tomorrow. You'll need a clear head."

"Me?"

"Yeh, you."

Chapter 12

Michael had never been able to come to terms with timekeeping. Time was like a bus that never stopped for him no matter how much he tried to flag it down. Timetables and the daily, clock-watching routines which helped most people through their day were mysteries to Michael. Watches were gifts you left for the next person who used the wash basin.

The following morning, as he sneaked into the flat to get Leo's breakfast, he should have known his father would be getting up to go to his new job and that his mother was due home from work, but these facts centred on TIME and they hadn't registered. Julia caught him stuffing a pound of cheese (was it all right for Jews to eat cheese?), a carton of spicy prawn mayonnaise dip (was it all right for Jews to eat prawn dip?), a frozen sliced loaf, and two yoghurts into a shopping bag.

Julia told Michael she was worried sick by his behaviour and insisted he tell her what was going on. Michael told her the food was for Leo Meyer. Julia thought it was all right for Jews to eat cheese, prawns probably not, and definitely not frozen bread and that he had to stop all this silliness right away and stay away from that man. Simon was very worried as well. Mr Meyer should be in hospital.

Michael's head was down. The sun, on what was going to be a very hot day, would defrost the bread and he didn't care what Simon Leighton thought. Michael wanted to run, get out of the cage. Leo was alone. He should be with the old man; he mustn't fail Leo Meyer.

"At least let me know where you're going, Michael!

It's not right the way you carry on and you and your father between you have got me at my wit's end."

If it gave him a key to get out of the flat, it was worth it. "You mustn't tell anyone else, the police, anyone. Promise."

Julia nodded and Michael told her.

"Breakin' and enterin'," Bob Brady said from the bedroom door behind Michael. He finished pulling his shirt on. "That's what that is."

Julia grabbed her son's arm as he pushed past her but couldn't hold on.

"It's that old Jew again, isn't it?" said Bob angrily and went into the kitchen to get his breakfast.

Julia was exhausted: four deliveries during the night including a breach birth. She rubbed the side of her neck. A strange rash had erupted there the previous day. A promise made in those circumstances wasn't really a promise; it was forced out of her. And besides, it was for his own good. He was only fifteen. She did worry about Michael. Maybe she didn't show it enough and maybe lately she had been spending a bit more time enjoying herself and not running around after the Brady men – the Brady boys – but that didn't mean that she didn't care. Julia picked up the telephone and dialled. She asked the hospital exchange to put her through to Simon Leighton's office.

J J slept uneasily, waking frequently during the night and finally, through exhaustion, oversleeping the time she had set herself for getting up. She dressed quickly, filled a shopping bag with food from the kitchen and rushed through her parents' office.

Margaret Pickles kept her gaze fixed on the VDU; a department of a multi-national oil company had made a tentative inquiry and if the Pickles Executive Search agency pitched its reply right, then it could secure a very lucrative contract.

"Going out, Joanna Jane?"

DON'T CALL ME THAT! J J didn't break her stride across the room, "Yeh, I'm guarding a survivor of the Nazi death camps. Someone's trying to kill him."

Her mother jerked her head back sharply from the screen: *was* *benefited* *spelt with one* *t* *or two?* Contracts could be won or lost on the strength of one's spelling.

"Well, if you remember, pick up some Earl Grey. We're right out."

★ ★ ★ ★ ★

"What is happening to us?"

Rashid was torn: there was such a gloomy atmosphere in the house that he thought he ought to stay and try to help his mother and father in some way. But he also wanted to go to the office block. He felt guilty, but Rashid admitted to himself that he was much more caught up in Leo Meyer's problems than in those of his own family. And besides, the two were beginning to overlap. He couldn't answer his father's question but he did know that the break-in the night before had something to do with the old man.

The police had just left, after a follow-up call to see if the Hassans had thought of anything else that had been stolen. They were puzzled; not much had been taken, but it hadn't the usual marks of a racist attack.

117

That is what Farouk believed it was. He tried to stay polite towards his son, but the boy's talk about the thugs wanting some of his photographs was nonsense, more proof that Rashid lived in some modern escapist world of his own where all that mattered were fast cars, expensive clothes and American films with far-fetched plots. He had forbidden him to talk to the police about it.

"You have to go to see Tahir," said Ellen quietly.

Farouk neither said nor did anything in reply but Rashid knew that his father, looking weak, vulnerable, smaller, would swallow his pride and go.

★ ★ ★ ★ ★

Away from uniforms and institutions, Leo Meyer had slept well and woke hungry enough to eat cheese and spicy prawn dip for his breakfast. He complimented Michael and the embarrassed boy disappeared behind his hair once more.

"You 'aven't got one of those numbers on your arm. I thought they all 'ad them… in them camps."

"I had it removed."

"Why?"

"I was ashamed."

Michael didn't know what to reply. He couldn't understand why anyone who survived the Nazi concentration camps should feel that way – they should be heroes of some sort – but he didn't want to upset Leo by asking more questions. He rose, forced four slices of frozen bread apart and placed them in the sun on the window sill.

118

Leo watched the dark, silent boy, watched his quick, twitchy, movements; his animal, ever-wary alertness and saw a victim who was learning to survive, like those in the camp who had very special hiding places and who turned up at the end of each day with an extra half-ration of bread, a small potato, a patched vest or a bartered spoon.

The others soon appeared, the Asian boy who knew that bullies had to be defeated and the girl who was so active and inquisitive, so demanding. *Tell the police.* Leo had to get back to the fox. He pushed the sleeping bag from him, tried to stand but slipped back to the floor. Nothing was steady any more and a wave of sickness washed over him. He closed his eyes and, for a moment, was standing docilely in the mud of the roll-call square with the others, grey, emaciated, stupid pyjama uniform, heads down, not looking at the gallows or at the sneering, superior face of Obersturmbannführer Scheffler. The trapdoor flapped open and another kitchen thief was punished. He, Leo Meyer, had accepted it then and for fifty years had continued to accept, had remained a grey, docile figure, only half a man, always looking down. From him, the enemy had nothing to fear. And now these children were telling him it could be otherwise.

J J took some cereal and milk from her shopping bag but Leo politely refused more breakfast. Rashid went to the window once again. He was nervous and wanted to get out of the building. He didn't like being there. J J noticed.

"Thought you preferred the city?"

"When things are normal and when we're doing normal things, I do."

The streets of Brancaster's main shopping centre were filling quickly that morning. It was a very hot day. Summer sales were opening at one of the large department stores and a rock group was making a promotional visit to a record shop. Rashid looked up York Street and saw, over the crest of the hill, the roofs of the indoor markets. In his mind, he saw one shuttered unit standing like a tombstone in the middle of the morning briskness of those markets. Rashid wondered if it would ever open again. Perhaps he'd even let his dad persuade him to wear some of the clothes from the stall if it did.

His eyes followed the van along the one-way system as it came from St John's Lane, down York Street, past the queue of young people outside the record store, through the pedestrian lights that were winking orange, and around the long bend into Westgate. It was barely a hundred metres from Churchill Tower before Rashid realised he was looking at the same white Ford Transit that he had seen outside his house and at the bus station.

Rashid's first reaction was to back away from the window immediately and warn the others, but a faint pulse of recognition beat in his vision and held him where he was. The driver: it was the moustache; that moustache like two slugs that had crawled up the chin and met above the mouth. He broke his gaze, crossed to the desk and dragged Michael to the window: "Just stupid, your dad, is he?"

The Transit was in the forecourt, Jake Gillery and his friends spilling out the back before Bob Brady brought it to a halt.

"What's this all about anyway? Nobody's goin' to gerr

'urt, are they?" he asked Avril. She brought a smile slowly to her carefully made-up face. When she spoke, it was a different Avril to the bubbly, flirtatious woman who had put him at ease on his first day at the garage.

"We only hurt those who oppose our cause and then, only when absolutely necessary."

Brady reached to turn the ignition off.

"Don't!" Avril snapped. "Turn the van round and keep the engine running."

Bob Brady did as he was told.

Michael got Leo to his feet. The old man protested. He was still tired and besides, he joked, there was still some of that spicy prawn dip to eat. The Asian boy stood right in front of him.

"You want to defeat the bullies, don't you?"

Leo smiled – *the children as teachers* – and nodded agreement. Yes, he wanted to defeat the bullies.

J J was thinking hard. "If we get into the shops and the crowds, they'll never get us."

"And then what?"

J J was irritated by Rashid's question. She hesitated. J J, the impetuous one, the one who rushed, over-confident, like a bull at a gate, suddenly faced the reality of what was happening and it scared her. She realised that, until that moment, it had been a game to her, a holiday adventure that had drawn them into a puzzling adult world. As the puzzle was disentangled, J J understood how threatening that world was and also how much was being asked of her. The bossy, cheeky J J had always tried to lead. It was expected of her now.

"Then we'll buy you a new comb. Your hair's a state."

Rashid realised he hadn't combed his hair that morning, the first time he had forgotten since he was ten. And he also realised that he wasn't bothered. It could stay a mess. There were more important things to worry about. He laughed, gave J J a quick hug and then told her to move herself.

The thugs entered by the front door and moved methodically through the building from the bottom upwards. The steady rhythm of the search, the military thump of the running steps along the corridors, of doors opened and shut, shouts, steps along corridors once more, froze the young people in indecision for a moment as they left Michael's "office".

Michael pointed to the right and led them down a back staircase to a service entrance and an underground car park. Leo could only shuffle slowly, but they were soon out of Churchill Tower and into the busy city shopping centre.

Jake found the deserted hideout on the third floor and angrily swept an arm across the desk scattering the remains of Michael's makeshift breakfast to the floor: "Jew pigswill!" From the window, he saw the kids hurrying Leo Meyer up York Street, the girl looking behind regularly.

Chapter 13

Leo wanted to be defiant, wanted to do what these young people asked, but he had to stop. The hill, the people bumping into him, the heat, his legs which kept telling him they didn't know how to walk, it was all too much. He stopped. The girl urged him on. The dark-skinned boy told her to take it easy. The other one took his arm.

"You'll get your second wind soon."

Second wind! What was the child talking about. Getting his first wind was the problem! Leo walked five yards more and stopped again.

"A moment," he gasped. "Just one moment. Don't worry, I am not *Musselman*."

Musselman puzzled them. Michael made a strongman pose, bending his arm at the elbow. "Muscleman?" Leo smiled at him, Michael, the survivor.

J J kept looking back towards Churchill Tower and scanning the crowds to spot any pursuers. She was certain that their group would be seen easily: three young people and a frail, elderly man stopping, starting, an odd presence in the crowd, like a bright, plastic shopping bag in a country stream. They had almost reached the record store. A few more steps, J J pleaded, and then they could pretend they were part of the queue waiting to get a glimpse of the five-member, heavy metal group, *Kevin*.

They helped Leo to the queue. He was wheezing loudly when they stopped again. He had to have a rest. Four girls in front of them stopped chattering and jiggling with excitement when they saw the old man. They looked Leo up and down, pulled faces, chewed loudly and open-mouthed for a moment and then started chattering and jiggling again.

"I 'ope Gary's there."

"They're all there, stupid."

"Gary's gorgeous."

"'e's 'ad 'is 'air cut."

"'e 'an't, 'as 'e?"

"'e 'as."

"Don' know if ah'll like 'im as much wid 'is 'air cut."

J J turned away muttering, "Daft tarts," to herself but worrying that they hadn't gone far enough and had been spotted. She looked at the floods of people on both sides of the road. She wanted to escape, of course, but she also wanted to pick one of the pursuers out; identify a face from the photographs, see one of them in the flesh come towards her, perhaps see him smiling and apologising, explaining there had been a stupid mistake, that things weren't as they seemed. She shivered in spite of the heat. Such thoughts were silly. People hurt other people. These people could hurt them.

"They'll hurt us, won't they?" J J asked Leo quietly.

Leo's face crumpled and for a moment it seemed he might cry. That "us", two insignificant letters, became a wonderful, sensuous snake of meaning that uncoiled itself, reached for his heart and pulled him towards the girl. "Us"... family... community. Leo realised he wanted to be a part of them again; he wanted to belong. But belonging meant your troubles visited others.

"Yes," he answered, "they will hurt us."

Michael pulled at J J's shoulder and pointed back down the hill.

"Maroon top: 'e's one of them."

It was the man who had been with his dad in the pub

on the evening they had found Leo in the wood. Jake Gillery and the others had spread out across the street and were moving steadily through the crowd. J J saw the one Michael pointed out. He wasn't smiling and didn't look as if he wanted to apologise.

"Into the store!"

The queue was getting restless. It was past the time they had been told they would see *Kevin*. The publicity shots and interviews were taking longer than planned. They began to surge in a good-humoured way towards the entrance. Two rows of heavy, unsmiling security guards held them back. Michael pulled Leo behind him, forcing a way through. People shouted and tried to block his path, but Rashid and J J, following close behind, held them back and explained that the old man was ill and had to lie down.

"Pull the other one!"

When they reached the doors, a guard took one look at Leo and let them through into the store. The usual long rows of stacking units densely packed with CDs, LPs and cassette tapes had been pushed back to create a central space where *Kevin* were posing with their instruments and copies of the new album, *Wipe it Up*. Banks of photographers and journalists surrounded them.

"This way, Mark!" Mark, the bassist, turned, stuck his tongue out and wiggled it. Cameras flashed. "Great!"

"Gary, one more, please!" Gary, the drummer, pushed the end of one of his sticks into a nostril. Cameras flashed. "Great!"

Another group might have distracted her, thought J J, but not *Kevin*, a three-chord, sexist, heavy metal group.

"What do we do now?" Rashid asked. "We're trapped

in here."

"I don't know. I'm thinking," J J snapped back. She saw Jake talking with one of the men on the door. The man was smiling, laughing. They seemed to know each other. Jake was pointing at her and the man was letting him through. Jake patted him on the shoulder, and mouthed, "Cheers". Four other men followed him.

J J grabbed a CD of *Wipe it Up* and told Rashid to give her some money.

"I don't like *Kevin*."

"Give it to your girlfriend then."

"Very funny." Rashid pulled a five pound note and some coins out of his pocket, not enough to buy the CD. Michael shrugged his shoulders. He had no money.

"It'll have to be the single, then," said J J, grabbing money from Rashid and handing it to an assistant behind the counter. "Let's introduce ourselves."

Kev, lead singer of *Kevin*, looked puzzled when he saw Leo Meyer and the others standing in front of him. He chewed, nodded, gave them a sleepy smile and said, "Yeh, great."

"Your biggest fan," said J J. "Discharged himself from hospital so he could be here."

"Great, yeh, great."

The strangeness of what was happening seemed to stir new life in Leo. He laughed, "I have everything you have ever recorded, right from your early days with Heifetz."

Kev looked puzzled again, but nodded and smiled and said, "Brilliant."

The photographers started to dismantle their equipment. Jake burst through them, knocking a tripod over. An angry photographer grabbed him and told him he should be more careful. Jake pushed him off easily but was rocked by a punch from someone behind him. A fight broke out. Several of the security men left the doors and ran across. The fed-up girls at the front of the queue outside saw their opportunity and rushed the thin line of guards that remained. They broke through easily and hundreds raced after them through the gap, screaming and spreading like quicksilver over the shop interior.

"Sign, please," J J pushed the single into Kev's hands but pulled Leo past him and past Gary and his drums towards an emergency exit at the back of the store. Rashid ran ahead, forced the bar-release down, and pushed the door open. With Leo half-laughing, half-coughing, they left the store.

J J turned right into the narrow access lane at the back of the store and down the slope in the direction of Churchill Tower. Doubling-back on their route up York Street seemed a good idea. The thugs wouldn't expect them to do that. A huge, white delivery lorry almost blocked the lane totally. They squeezed against the walls to get past. Rashid scuffed his jacket badly on some rough cast but didn't care.

When they were fifty metres beyond the lorry, the Transit van entered the bottom of the lane and was driven fast towards them. They turned to go back the way they had come but a grinning Jake emerged from the side of the lorry. Rashid pointed to an open door across the lane, where someone was sitting outside, half-dozing in the tar-bubbling heat. It was an employees' entrance to one of the George Street shops that backed on to the lane. Jake saw what they were going to do and started to run. The rest of the gang spilled out from behind the lorry and raced after him.

JJ stepped around the sleepy shop assistant and into a stockroom full of books, magazines, and newspapers, many still bound or shrink-wrapped. Michael and Rashid followed, half-carrying Leo. Rashid kicked over several stacks hoping this would slow down their pursuers. The assistant was startled out of his catnap by the noise. Jake reached him as he got to his feet and pushed him back down again.

JJ led them into the sales area and, weaving in and out of customers, walked rapidly along a whole wall of magazines that told her how she should be running her life: *Smart Girls Get More!... Moving in with Your Lover... Bright Girl Fashion... Me... Breast Implants... How to Keep Your Man... How Far Would You Go for the Body Beautiful? Multiple...* past the cash desk and through the automatic doors on to George Street. Leo shuffled as quickly as he could between Michael and Rashid. They heard more crashes and swearing in the stockroom before they were outside once more with JJ.

Breathing hard and holding on to Michael, Leo told them that he couldn't go much further. JJ didn't want them to stop there. "Just a bit more. Through the car park..." She pointed. "And down to Cathedral Gardens. We should be well away from them by then." Leo shook his head.

"Mek a chair," Michael said. He crossed his arms. Rashid saw what he meant, crossed his arms and gripped Michael's hands tightly. They bent low and eased Leo on to the "chair". Leo put his arms around their shoulders. JJ told them to hurry. Through the shop doors, she saw a shop assistant trying to stop Jake.

Slowly, J J, Rashid, Michael and Leo crossed George Street into the largest multi-storey car park in Brancaster, a grey concrete block that was like a crudely filled tooth among its Victorian sandstone neighbours. It was good to be out of the glare and noise of the streets. There was something reassuring in the gloom of the low-ceilinged car park and in the steady swish, swish of tyres as cars spiralled steadily upwards to the different levels. They allowed themselves a few smiles. Leo stepped off his chair. Rashid put his arm around J J's shoulder. No one saw the man stalking them behind a row of cars until he crossed in front of them to cut off the exit to the Cathedral Gardens. He spoke into his walkie-talkie.

* * * * *

Bob Brady drove the van up the ramp to the first level of the car park. They'd never catch them, he was sure: a van chasing kids on foot around the streets? Never, even with the old man. But he wouldn't say owt. Just keep quiet, do what he was told and sort out Michael at home that evening.

Rashid saw the van first. He took his arm off J J's shoulder, ran through the parked cars to the lift, hoping it was working, and frantically banged on the call button. J J helped Leo into a piggy-back position on Michael's back and they went after Rashid. The lift was working; Rashid, ear pressed to the metal doors could hear the faint whirring of the mechanism answering his call. But it was slow, very slow and the van was closing on them. The lift arrived with a thud and a bell rang. The van screeched to a halt. There was an agonising wait – one second, two seconds, three. Two men leapt from the back of the van and sprinted towards them. Four, five seconds – the doors opened. Rashid held them back at one side while the others stepped into the lift and then there was another four seconds that seemed like forty before the doors closed just as one of the thugs was reaching forward to grab them. As they rose up the lift shaft to the roof, Leo, J J, Michael and Rashid heard his angry, futile thumping on the doors below them.

J J was very quiet in the lift. The others were running, behaving instinctively in trying to get away from their pursuers and doing what she told them to do. The burden had been on her to think ahead and she now realised her thinking had led them to a dead end. She had brought them into the car park and now they were heading for the roof. Once they were on the roof, what could they do? Parachute into the street? Hire a helicopter? Ask the thugs to kindly stop chasing them? They were trapped. J J apologised. Rashid put his arm around her again and told her it would be all right. Leo said the same. Michael looked down at the floor of the lift.

The doors seemed to open even more slowly at the top of the lift shaft. They heard the van's tyres squealing on the bends one level below.

"The lift. Back down." suggested Michael.

J J tried to slow her racing thoughts down. "They'll have someone at the doors," she said.

"We've got to do something!" shouted Rashid.

Three of the thugs came running up the roadway on to the far end of the roof. The van emerged right behind them and stopped. The runners talked to the woman in the passenger seat, then spread out and started to walk

130

steadily the length of the roof, checking in between the cars. J J and the others hid behind the lift shaft and then, crouching, moved in pairs: Michael and Leo, J J and Rashid, among the cars towards the parapet at the opposite end of the roof. Once there, they had nowhere else to go. Leo slumped to the ground, exhausted, his back against a C-class Mercedes, and said he was going to give himself up and they wouldn't be harmed.

"What now?"

J J looked at Rashid to see if he was criticising her. He wasn't. It was a genuine plea for her to come up with an idea. The three of them looked through the car windows to see where their hunters were. They had reached the lift and one of them stayed there cutting off that line of escape. Rashid stroked the car door. His uncle Tahir drove one of these.

"Beautiful machine."

J J had spotted something but said nothing. She didn't need to. Michael had noticed the same thing and knew what she was thinking. The keys were dangling from the ignition.

"I stopped tekkin' cars ages ago. You know that."

"Well, you can start again. This is an emergency."

Jake was pointing their way. He had seen Rashid ducking back down behind the car. They didn't rush. No need to. The kids and the old Jew were trapped.

Michael looked at the exhausted Leo. The old man waved a hand before his eyes, a dismissive gesture, "Go, leave me." That was the last thing Michael Brady was going to do.

"You get 'im in!"

Still keeping low, Michael opened the driver's door and

got in. Rashid and J J helped Leo into the spacious back seat. J J was closing the door when Michael started the engine. Michael tried to calm himself; his thoughts were going all ways at once. Some took him back over a year to a giddy, stupid, frightening time when he'd stolen cars almost every night and raced them over lonely moor roads. He put the car into Drive and, out of nervousness, accelerated hard. Tyres squealing and exhaust smoking, the Mercedes made a furious racing start from the parking space and almost hit a ticket machine.

"Follow the arrows!" screamed J J.

Michael did, but he followed them the wrong way, speeding past the Transit van and down the roadway it had just come up. J J reached over and held her hand on the horn as they corkscrewed down the levels, swerving wildly and missing by a hair's breadth cars ascending the building. Michael pulled the Mercedes on to the second floor and found arrows pointing him the right way. J J flopped into the back seat. As Michael, braking softly, took the car into the wide curve to Level One and the exit, he glimpsed the van in his rear-view mirror.

"They're right behind!"

Michael turned right out of the car park and dropped down Cathedral Hill. As he did so, a red Sierra pulled in sharply to block the car park exit, and a tall, unkempt man in an ill-fitting dark blue suit got out, raised the bonnet and peered at the engine.

Chapter 14

Leo would make no decisions about going to the police until he had been home. He needed time to think. J J: "You've had fifty years!" Rashid: "Shut up, J J!"

The children didn't understand: fifty years, a hundred years wasn't long enough. How did one speak about such things? Language was a babbling baby. And how did you stop your heart from bursting with the horror of the memories or your conscience from crippling you with guilt? Go to the police. A walk through a door, a chat; that's all it was to the children. To Leo Meyer, revealing who he was, identifying the real Scheffler and testifying, would bring back into sharp focus those three years in Gehenna and he was not sure he could bear that.

The farmhouse, he insisted. The fox had to be fed and there were things he needed.

"We can't stay here long. It's one of the places they're bound to check. Maybe the cave…" J J noticed the slight waver in her voice and told herself not to panic. That was hard since she no longer felt in control. She was being carried along by events and reacting to things as they happened. The cave seemed a good idea for a hiding place until they could get Leo to see sense. Adults wouldn't think of looking there.

"Michael, you've got to get rid of the car. They'll be looking for it, and the police. If we're not here when you get back, we'll be in the cave… I'll feed the fox. Rash, get some blankets and things and keep an eye on Leo."

Rashid almost gave a stiff-arm, Nazi response but stopped himself and settled for a more conventional salute. J J and Michael left and he helped Leo into his shabby armchair.

The very hungry fox was turning, turning in its pen. Its leg seemed to have mended completely. J J fed it quickly and ran back through the wood. Although traffic was rare on that road, she stopped automatically at the edge of the trees and looked both ways. J J laughed at her extreme caution, but as she crossed, her eyes tripped on something glinting in the wood further along the road. On the other side, she headed towards the farmhouse for twenty metres, then pushed into the tall bracken and walked back to a spot directly opposite whatever had caught the sun's rays. It was the red Sierra parked well into the wood and it was empty. Rashid! J J picked up a length of broken fencing and, keeping to the road, ran as fast as she could back to the house.

Well-quarried, chipped, broken, extracted, crudely filled, Yaakov Epstein's teeth looked like partly demolished rows of houses. He revealed them in a broad, messy smile as he bent over the dozing Leo Meyer.

Rashid came back from the kitchen at the same time as J J burst through the front door screaming his name. Keeping the smile, Yaakov looked up at the boy and put a hand into a bulging jacket pocket. A breathless J J almost fell into the living room, her eye drawn immediately to the man's hand which was gripping a long object in the pocket and beginning to withdraw it. The big man, the one who had been creeping around close to them ever since they had found Leo, started to turn towards her. J J didn't hesitate. She had spent too many rainy winter Saturday afternoons watching Cagney, Raft and Bogart ruin double-breasted suits to do that. She took one...

134

two… three steps, swung the fence post and felled Yaakov Epstein.

Panting heavily, J J stood over the big man. He groaned and rolled over on to his face. Leo shifted in his chair, muttered something but didn't open his eyes. J J looked down at what she had done, let go of the club as if it was red hot and brought both hands to her face. It wasn't like on the films at all: that crack as the wood hit the side of his skull, his moaning. She couldn't catch her breath. She was going to cry. Rashid was stunned. He couldn't believe what had happened. He moved to J J's side and held her.

"It's all right. You had to do it."

"I had to… He was…"

"Yeh, I know."

"In his pocket… you could've been…"

"It's all right… You had to do it… but… but…" Humour, thought Rashid, might bring them both round. "But your wrist action wasn't right. It wouldn't have gone for four."

J J looked at him, puzzled. Rashid picked up the length of wood. "A square cut should be more like this. See, the wrists."

J J smiled and made an effort to gather her breath and emotions. She shook her head and play-punched him.

"Cricket. At a time like this."

Rashid hugged her again, but quickly let go and bent over the big man. "He's going to be in action again soon. We've got to do something."

"Like a straight drive or something, you mean?" J J giggled and then felt tears welling again. It was all too much especially when she saw Rashid pull several bars of chocolate from the man's "gun" pocket.

135

Before he came round, J J and Rashid bound and gagged the intruder. J J went through all his pockets but found only more chocolate bars and the keys to the Sierra.

The interior of his car didn't explain much to them. It was fitted with a CB radio and there were some documents written in a strange language. Rashid reached under the fascia panel and ripped out all the wires he could find while J J investigated a box on the back seat. It contained more bars of chocolate.

A heavy summer shower started. J J shouted, competing with the rain on the car roof: "We've got to get away from the house now! The others'll be here soon when they don't hear from him."

When he stepped out of the Mercedes, Michael felt as if he had just been set free after ten years' solitary confinement. Every junction, he had been sure, would bring a police patrol car into the rear-view mirror and that would mean he wouldn't get back to Leo. He had to get back to Leo.

Michael left the car, with the keys under a front wheel, at the bottom of Birch Lane, on the edge of the city centre restricted parking zone and telephoned the police to tell them. Then Michael was off, running, past the blackened Yorkshire stone of the old mills and warehouses – *I LOVE YOU SHAHZEERA* – past the unofficial tipping sites with their rotting mattresses and rusting washing machines. Michael was content; happier than he had been for a long time because he had something he wanted to do, a mission to look after Leo Meyer and make sure no one hurt him. Not even the memory of his father driving the thugs' van was troubling him. He decided to go straight up Birch Lane, along Nelson Avenue, and on to the Moor Road. From there, he could be back at the farmhouse in under an hour if he took Whitemonk path, a shortcut to Hangman's Rocks.

He slowed to a jog – had to save some energy for the steep climb up Whitemonk – as he passed Simpson's, the biggest of the abandoned mills. Its windows were boarded up and hung with posters.

NEW HARVEST! TO HEAL YOUR BODY,
SET YOU FREE FROM YOUR HABITS
AND DO MIRACLES IN YOUR LIFE!

A short, drenching summer shower started just before Araf's gang stepped out of the mill yard and grabbed him. Michael shouted, screamed about Leo, how he had to get back to Leo, that they were trying to kill him, the fascists; kill an old Jew. No one in the gang spoke. They blindfolded him and dragged him into the mill. Araf was waiting at the top of the stone stairs. When someone pulled the scarf roughly from his eyes and Michael saw the drop below him, he almost fainted.

"Can't… tek…" Everything was moving like a crazy fairground ride: the landing he stood on melted; the mill walls heaved inwards; the huge girders swayed. Michael's head was a thick soup of dizziness. "… stand… 'eights."

Imran stepped forward and steadied him.

"Don't help that guy! He's trespassed on our territory once too often."

Imran ignored Araf and pulled Michael back from the edge. "What fascists?" he asked him quietly.

137

Michael breathed deeply. He saw genuine sympathy in Imran's eyes. "They've gorra van... white... was blue... Ford Transit." Michael looked around slowly. Everyone was on the landing. Only Imran could stop Michael making a run for it back down the stairs. Imran knew what he was thinking and, unseen by the rest of the gang, he smiled and nodded gently when Michael's eyes caught his once more. Michael pushed him and ran wildly down the three flights of stairs and back out on to Birch Lane. Some of the gang started to go after him but Imran stood in their way. Araf was furious.

"Like who's in charge round here, Imran?"

Imran smiled at him.

★ ★ ★ ★ ★

Farouk regretted coming the moment he stepped into Tahir's clean, bare office. However, he had promised Ellen he would speak to his brother about their money problems and that's what he would do.

Tahir stayed behind his desk and talked finance for a while: equities; annuities; bonds; trusts; balanced investment strategies and the current volatility of the market. Farouk became impatient. His brother knew why he had come. There was no need for all this talk. Farouk interrupted him.

"A loan with proper interest rates charged; a straightforward business deal. Do not think of me as your brother."

Tahir looked out of the window. One of his best clients was withdrawing money from the cashpoint at the National Bank of Pakistan. He made a mental note to contact him about his unit trust portfolio.

"You *are* my brother, Farouk. Were you someone off the street, I would not know your history and could respond to your request favourably…"

Farouk should have gone then. He had hoped to find some simple humanity in his brother's response.

"Oil and water don't mix, Farouk. An English proverb and a very useful one. But you think otherwise and you have betrayed your people. The community has to be kept intact, pure; there is so much here that corrupts. I cannot be seen in any way to condone your marriage outside of the community. It is my moral duty to refuse to help you."

Farouk was on his way to the door before his brother had finished. He did not say a word more. On the street outside, he stopped and took a deep breath. The air was fresher and the light above the house tops clearer after the shower. Farouk doubted if he would ever return to his brother's office or his house, but the thought did not upset him. He felt strangely happy and free. He and Ellen would manage. They always had.

Chapter 15

When Yaakov Epstein freed himself, the first thing he did was eat two Mars Bars. Then he wandered slowly about Leo Meyer's house, opening drawers, cupboards, riffling through the few books he found, searching pockets in the old man's clothes, and sometimes simply touching surfaces. He wanted to know, really know Leo Meyer. Yaakov had studied their life histories and had met many Jews who had suffered in the camps. Few were alike in the ways they had come to terms with those terrible experiences: there were the quiet workers, the ones who recorded everything, determined to bear witness; there were some who revelled in the beauty of a life lived in freedom; there were the militants who sought retribution in any way possible from the hunting down of war criminals to the refusal to buy anything German; there were the constantly agitated ones, who relived the camps and their emotions daily; there were those who tried to draw curtains on those years, who said; "I was there. I had enough." There were also those like Meyer, whose lives were apologies for surviving, but none who, in Yaakov's experience, carried so much guilt and demanded so much self-mortification.

In the front room, Yaakov pored over Leo's collection of cuttings on the death camps, noting in particular the references to Bunkers I and II at Auschwitz. Yaakov nodded knowingly. His researches had already told him that Leo's father had been conscripted into the work parties that had converted those Polish peasant farmhouses into Auschwitz's first gas chambers. More guilt, from father to son. Yaakov switched the tape recorder to play and, at full volume, a familiar voice, full of fury and menace, strutted through the small house.

Yaakov listened for a moment and pictured the scene at Nürnberg: the forest of proud flags; the flaming torches; the thousands in uniform marching in perfect step to one man's whim. Noises interrupted Yaakov's thoughts. Above the voice, he heard a car door banging, heavy boots on the garden path and the front door being smashed open. He dashed from the room. In a cupboard under the stairs, he covered himself with old sacking and bit quietly into a bar of Fruit and Nut. One... two... three... four... four of them tore through the small house, looking for the "stinking Jew". Hitler's passionate oratory followed them.

He stopped chewing. One of them was right outside the cupboard. The man was out of condition. Yaakov heard a slight wheeze in his heavy breathing and then a curse as the man caught his finger on the jagged latch. Yaakov stiffened, dropped the Fruit and Nut – "Damn!" – and tried to prepare himself for the struggle that seemed likely. There wasn't much time and the karate lessons were a faint memory. Don't tense. Relax; be serene. Breathing, proper breathing was important, Yaakov remembered; proper breathing and concentration on one's *hara*, the spiritual and physical focal point just below the navel. His mouth was full of chocolate: he couldn't breathe as he was supposed to do. His mind wasn't focused either; he was wondering where the bar of Fruit and Nut had fallen. Chocolate was ruining him.

The wheezing thug opened the small door a few inches, but that was all. Yaakov heard names being called. He made a mental note of them: Gary, Brad, Robbo. They were being called to do something else. "From the moor," he heard and then they were silent. In the front room, Hitler's speech finished in mid-sentence as the reel ran out and the only sound Yaakov heard was the soft, slap, slap of the loose end of the tape. He slumped back down under the sacking and pulled a Double Decker from his inside pocket.

* * * * *

Michael had run most of the way down the moorside from Hangman's Rocks and was out of breath. Something wasn't right. He walked cautiously through the garden to the front door. Why weren't J J and Rashid watching for him? Why had the tape been playing? He moved slowly around the outside of the house peering in at the dirty windows. It looked empty.

Michael had decided to go straight to the cave when a woman came round a corner of the house and greeted him with a big smile, a false smile, the kind nurses gave you when they wanted you to take the needle like "a brave little soldier." She told him she was Leo's niece and asked if Michael had any idea where her uncle was. She was in the area for the day only and would love to see him.

Michael recognised her from the car park, remembered the fury in her face as he'd raced the Mercedes the wrong way past the van. Avril advanced slowly towards him saying she hoped Uncle Leo hadn't upset him in any way: "You know, he's had a rough life. Got some strange ideas."

Michael backed off, then turned to run, slipped on the wet grass and was grabbed.

* * * * *

Bob Brady was seeing things a bit more clearly now and felt, well, not happy about what was happening and his part in it, but a bit calmer. As long as they didn't ask him to do anything other than some driving – he wasn't into all the strong arm stuff – then he'd go along with them. He looked straight in front of him through the windscreen. He wanted to know as little as possible about what the rest of them were doing. "Park behind the house and wait," Avril had said and that's what he was doing. Michael was stupid to get involved with the old guy.

Jake banged on the door and waved for him to shift the van. He reversed from the back of the house on to the road and glanced quickly into his rear-view mirror. Couldn't see much really. The old guy; yeh, that's who they were after. Not interested in the kids, Avril had said. Could be old. Being dragged, stumbling, saying nothing, probably gagged. Bag over his head; into the van; jammed between Jake and Robbo. Bob kept quiet. Yorkshire Man's philosophy: *Hear all, see all, say nowt. Eat all, sup all, pay nowt. And if ever tha' does owt for nowt, allus do it for thi'sen.*

Best policy, Bob told himself, and everything will be fine. Yeh, Avril had said they weren't interested in the kids. And Avril was OK. Bit bossy about this Group 88 business, but OK. Got things done. Bit of life to her, not like some women he could name. One woman. The country going to be knackered if somebody didn't do something about foreigners. The old man was a threat, that's what she'd said, a threat to the security of the whole

144

Movement. Don't let his age fool you. Still, you couldn't help being a bit nervous. What were they going to do with the old guy, anyway? An end-job? Just drive the bloody van, Bob Brady, he told himself. Don't ask questions.

Number 2 bay door of Turner's Garage was drawn upwards into its overhead position as the van approached. Avril was the only one who had spoken on the way back from Brereton Moor and then only once to say that *he* wouldn't be pleased. The rest of the journey passed in silence: voices could be recognised; keep communication to a minimum.

Bob Brady kept telling himself that it wasn't Michael. His surreptitious glances in the rear-view mirror told him nothing. Whoever it was was being forced to keep his head between his knees. When he pulled to a stop inside the bay, Bob had a decision to make and that was whether or not to find out if it was his son. He sat at the wheel while everyone else got out. Robbo and Brad dragged the captive from the van. There was a struggle. They hit him, dull thuds – one, two, three – about the body, each followed by a low, animal whimper that Bob Brady recognised immediately, a cry that had irritated him so often and urged him on to hit the boy another time to shut his bloody whining up! He had to look. He stepped down from the driver's seat quickly and walked to the back of the van. Avril stopped him there. The prisoner was being pulled into a small office.

"You've done the driving, Brady. I'm pleased. You can leave the rest to us."

Bob nodded meekly and turned to head back towards

Reception. The bag had still been over his head, but the shape of the back, bent, as if flinching from another blow, and the size of feet that had overtaken his Dad's two years previously, told him it was Michael.

Jake came into Reception ten minutes later, pulling on overalls.

"We 'ave some fun, don't we?"

"It's our Michael, isn't it?"

Jake nodded. "'E knows where the old man is and 'e won't tell us. Leaves us with two options, that does. We can 'urt 'im and mek 'im tell us or we can bring the old man 'ere by threatening to 'urt 'im."

Bob moved forward to pass Jake, "I'll have a word wi' 'im. 'E'll listen to me."

Jake grabbed his arm. "Naw, don't do that, Bob. And don't worry, cos we're going for the second option. And this is where you can be a big 'elp. You're going to find 'is mates; the girl and that Paki. Get 'em to carry a message to the old guy. They 'and 'im over: your lad doesn't get 'urt."

★ ★ ★ ★ ★

… the fascists… kill the old Jew… a van… white… was blue… Ford Transit…

The sun had set when Imran woke with Michael's words still tumbling about his mind. The old lady who had been studying him through the Mini window straightened up and walked on when she saw him stir. Imran tried to stretch his long legs but the Mini didn't give much room for that. He had parked on Alma, the first of the crowded terraces of small houses – Alma,

146

Sebastapol, Inkerman, Balaclava – that sloped steeply down to Herse Road and overlooked one side and the back entry to Turner's Garage. From there, he had kept watch for most of the afternoon. What Michael Brady had said in Simpson's Mill had convinced him that the garage was the headquarters of Group 88, the thugs behind the fire-bombings and beatings.

Garage business had gone on normally, dully, the only excitement being a brief, breaktime game of soccer that a lone mechanic had played on the access road at the back. The Transit van returned; the employees, in ones and twos, left during the late afternoon. Nothing suspicious happened and Imran had fallen asleep. To waken himself up properly before driving home, he opened the driver's door and uncoiled himself outside. He looked down at the garage once more. From the thick band of light at the bottom, he realised that the far bay door, the one that had been raised for the Transit, was not locked.

There was just enough room for Imran to squeeze under. His heart raced: saying that he was after new tyres for the Mini wouldn't get him out of this. He heard voices and a radio playing. He could also hear noises from elsewhere in the garage. Someone was checking the lights and doors and activating the burglar alarms. He stayed on his hands and knees and crawled towards the van. Lying on his back, he unclasped his penknife and scratched at the paintwork on the driver's side sill: *white… was blue.*

* * * * *

J J and Rashid had made a comfortable nest of blankets

on a low, dry ledge halfway into the cave. Leo slept while they waited anxiously for Michael to join them.

Mama?

"*Close your eyes, Leo. You too, Miriam. Pretend you are safe in the forest and above the soaring trees you can see a thousand brilliant stars. Leo, stop fussing over that dog. Rest. It will be over soon.*"

But Mama, I hear them! They saw me, saw me with the dog! Mama, you must hear them too, their shouts, coward-shouts to give them courage to hunt children!

"*The stars, Leo. Look at the stars and hear the wind stroking the branches.*"

Mama, you must hear them, their boots stamping!

"*Which star is yours, Miriam? You want that one? It's a beautiful star. Your star and its light will never fade.*"

Mama, they are beating the floor with their rifles! The dust, Mama. It's making me want to cough. Mama, they know we're here… They will take us, Mama, won't they, to those places you will only whisper of? Mama, I'm frightened. Mama, they have dogs too! Mama, they're ripping out the floorboards. And Mama, yes, yes, yes, I see the stars!

The vividness of the dream startled Leo from his sleep. "It's a beautiful night."

Leo screwed his eyes up and looked hard at J J as if he had never seen her before. The candlelight cast strange, fretted shadows on the irregularly cut wall of the cave behind her. He nodded and looked to the entrance that framed a stretch of the ridge opposite Brereton Moor and the darkening sky above it. A few stars were out.

"Quite cold," added Rashid. "Will you be warm

enough, Mr Meyer?"

Leo nodded again. So many memories. If only there was some simple operation that could sieve one's recollections, do away with the horror and keep the happiness, the beauty, the stars.

"No one will find you here," said J J.

Leo nodded, "You are very kind young people. I will be all right."

Rashid pulled at J J's arm. "We have to go. It's late."

"We have to look for Michael," J J told Leo.

Rashid felt his resentment of Michael begin to surface once again as J J expressed her concern. For a moment, he wanted to find fault with Michael; say that they shouldn't fuss about him, that he'd probably forgotten all about Leo Meyer, and was with his father and the other fascists. Rashid stopped himself. He knew such things weren't true. J J was right to worry and he was being selfish, wanting her to focus attention on him for a change. He tugged her sleeve again, but J J had more to say. She had to ask once more if Leo would go to the police, tell them about Auschwitz, tell them about Scheffler.

"How could my words make people understand the evil that was there? How could they? I was there but I don't understand it."

"Maybe they don't need to understand. Maybe they just need to know that it can happen."

Leo watched the two young people make their way to the cave entrance. The boy took the girl's hand. She seemed pleased at that. He called after them.

"Tomorrow. Ask me again tomorrow."

In spite of Rashid's tugging at her hand, J J turned.

149

"Your family all died in those camps, didn't they?"

Leo did not reply. His hand, shaking slightly, reached and snuffed out the candle.

"You're their only witness. They're listening."

Chapter 16

Rashid didn't want to call at Michael's house in case they confronted Bob Brady, but J J insisted. Bob wasn't there and neither was Michael. His mother, late for work, told them that Michael was probably just having another one of his nights away, that she worried about him, but that she had her own life to live and couldn't nursemaid the Brady menfolk for ever, and that she hoped they had stopped all that silliness with the old man. He was ill and should be in hospital. Simon Leighton was very concerned.

J J shouted after her that her husband was helping the people who wanted to kill Mr Meyer. Julia stopped at the door of the Morris Minor and turned. She could do without all this bother; kids had too many holidays, too much free time for their imaginations to go crazy.

"If I thought Bob Brady had the energy, I might believe you."

J J told him it would be all right, but Rashid walked her home. They talked about Leo Meyer, about war, about racism, about evil. "Evil's in all of us," said Rashid.

They kissed outside her front door, not a passionate kiss, but a *tender* one. Rashid put his hands on her waist and held himself slightly away from her. J J was happy that Rashid was… *tender* with her. She shied away slightly from using the word – it wasn't fashionable, sounded soppy, but was the one she wanted and the one that fitted. Rashid was tender and respectful of her, her body, her opinions. She liked Rashid, *liked* him a lot. The relationship would develop the way they decided.

Fashion and the magazines and films wouldn't tell her what to do. Through the fanlight above the front door, they saw the hall light go off and on, off and on.

Rashid kissed J J again and from behind the front door, Margaret Pickles heard her daughter tell the Asian boy that he was *really evil*.

Margaret Pickles wanted a TALK. J J knew, without doubt, that her mother wanted to talk about SERIOUS MATTERS. There was one sure sign. J J had been asked none of the trivial questions her mother – not wanting answers and never listening to any – usually asked:

Had a nice time, Joanna Jane?… Hmmm… Ice rink?… Hmmm… Get something to eat, did you?… Hmmm… With what'shisname, were you?… Hmmm…

There had been none of that, which meant that her mother wanted to talk about SERIOUS MATTERS. Another sign was the fact that her mother consulted J J on what she should wear that evening. It was late but a client had invited her and Mervyn to a night club and, well, it was all pertinent to the growth of the Pickles Executive Search Agency.

"Is this top a bit too… well… showy… Joanna Jane?"

DON'T CALL ME THAT!

J J glanced quickly at the pink, tie-front, georgette blouse: *mutton dressed as lamb*. "It's fine," she answered.

"Which earrings? These or these?"

"Yes."

"Which?"

Eeny, meany, miney, mo… "Em, those ones."

It made J J feel very uncomfortable. Her Mum had prompted mother and daughter chattiness with her – with her, J J, about dressing! – and that had to be a prelude to a talk about SERIOUS MATTERS. J J switched the television on. The News was halfway through; inflation, recession, monetary union.

Margaret Pickles held herself straight and looked at her top half in the mirror over the large, marble fireplace.

"That boy…"

"Yeh."

"He's not white."

"Nothing gets past you, does it, Mum?"

The war crimes trial was being mentioned; another survivor claimed to have identified Bauer as Scheffler from his features and his distinctive walk. The man had broken down while recounting the horrors he had witnessed at Auschwitz. J J tried to concentrate on the report, but her mind went back to Michael. He might be at the cave, guarding Leo. J J hoped so. Her mother was close to the mirror now. She had tied her hair up but stray wisps were troubling her.

"He seems… nice. Are you … em… seeing each other?"

"No, we close our eyes whenever we're together."

"You know exactly what I mean, Joanna Jane."

"Don't call me that!"

"It's your name."

"Sounds like a rag doll."

Margaret Pickles left the mirror and stood between her daughter and the television blocking out an horrific ziggurat of entangled bodies at a Nazi extermination camp.

"Well, that's as may be, but what about this Asian."

"*This Asian*'s called Rashid and he's a good friend. Is there a problem with his skin colour?"

"No, of course not, but your father and I both think you should… consider the… cultural differences."

"His mother's snow-white and anyway, I thought you liked Asian food?"

J J's mother tottered a little. The shoes were new and she didn't wear such high heels often. Behind her, the News had moved on to sport.

"We do. Your father's stomach can't take it on a regular basis, but that's…"

"Well, don't worry, Rashid and I won't invite you round too often."

"Oh, Joanna, I do wish I could talk sensibly with you."

"Yeh, so do I."

Half-an-hour after her parents had gone, the door bell rang. J J switched on the outside light and checked through the front room bay window to see who it was. Then she opened the door to a very agitated Bob Brady.

"I'd no idea it was 'im, 'onest. They said they only wanted the old man. Wouldn't touch any of you lot."

J J wasn't sure of his mood. He smelt of the pub, his eyes were wide and he kept flicking his tongue around his moustache as if cleaning up after eating. She didn't invite him in but he stepped over the threshold. J J backed off. "I'll get my father. He's just upstairs."

"No, no, don't do that. No parents. No police. Just you. You and the Asian."

"You work for them, don't you?"

"I never wanted any of this!"

"You told them about the photographs and Churchill Tower."

"Photographs? I wanted a job, that's all."

154

"Where's Michael?"

"Don't ask questions. They'll kill him."

★ ★ ★ ★ ★

"You know, I'm glad he didn't lend me the money." Farouk was carrying dishes to the sink.

Rashid, seated at the table, only half-heard his father. In his mind, he was still walking home with J J in the near-dark down Whitemonk Path and into Birch Lane's busy side streets. Some heads turned; some looks were antagonistic; some comments were passed. Rashid had kept hold of her hand. He had felt secure, insulated from anything others could do to hurt them, and wondered if it had been like that for his father and mother.

"He would have made me pay more than interest. He would have tried to break this family up and that's not on."

Ellen joined her husband, put an arm around his waist and said, "We'll manage, manage on our own."

Rashid got up from the table with his plates and playfully pushed between his parents to get to the sink.

"Mum's right," he said. "We'll manage. Uncle Tahir's a bully. We can do without him."

"You'll have to cut back on your fancy clothes," his mother told him.

Rashid smiled, "Not a problem, Mum. There's more important things." Ellen Hassan stepped back, her face expressing mock amazement. "Don't laugh, Mum, I mean it."

The telephone rang. It was J J for Rashid. "Very convenient," Farouk said and he handed his son the

155

phone. "Gets you out of doing the dishes."

It was a long time before J J slept and when she did it was only to slip into the shallowest doze. She and Rashid had agreed to meet at half-seven the following morning and cycle to the cave to tell Leo what had happened. Just before she dozed, J J tried to imagine a happy conclusion to the day that was to follow, with Michael and Leo Meyer free and the fascists in prison. *Eleven o'clock: be at the middle of the three public telephones at t'top of t'markets. Tell 'em where they can find the old man or they'll kill Michael. No funny business. If they smell the police or owt, our Michael's finished.*

Chapter 17

For the first time ever during a school holiday, J J was dressed and downstairs before her parents had occupied their office chairs. She booted up her mother's computer and left a message on the screen:

MICHAEL HELD HOSTAGE BY VICIOUS NEO-FASCIST GROUP WHO WANT ELDERLY AUSCHWITZ SURVIVOR IN RETURN FOR HIS RELEASE. THIS MAN CAN IDENTIFY THE REAL FRANZ SCHEFFLER AND BRING HIM TO TRIAL.

CAN'T SAY MORE SINCE MICHAEL'S LIFE WILL BE IN DANGER IF I DO. DON'T LET THIS INFORMATION INTERFERE WITH TODAY'S BUSINESS. LOVE, J J.

The weather was cooler. From the front door of Spring House, J J could see that low cloud had settled on the moor. Rashid was waiting at the bottom of the drive. He looked as if he had slept in his clothes and his hair stuck out in several places. J J tried to smooth it.

"Rough night?"

He nodded: "I couldn't stop thinking about the old man and Michael and… and us."

"We'd better concentrate on *them* this morning. OK?"

Rashid smiled and swung his bicycle round and started to mount. As he did so, a tall, extremely unkempt man, a couple of sizes too large for the dark blue suit he was wearing, walked swiftly up to him and gripped the handlebars.

"Please, I must talk to you."

It was the man they had left tied up at the farmhouse. His size, paleness; his wide-apart, dark-blue eyes and mouth of broken teeth were frightening. Rashid tried to wrench his bicycle from the man's grip but failed.

"My name is Yaakov Epstein. I work for the International War Crimes Research Centre, based in Geneva and New York."

Releasing the bicycle with one hand he pulled a transparent plastic wallet from his inside pocket and showed it to them.

"My identity card."

J J read: "Green Flag National Breakdown membership/ insurance number R.159…"

Yaakov snatched the card back: "I don't want to hurt your friend, Mr Meyer. I want to help him. Please believe me."

JUNE'S CORNER CAFE was small but busy. A couple of down-and-outs in grubby parkas and woollen hats were drinking tea and three gangs of building labourers were having large, fried breakfasts. Yaakov brought cups of coffee and a selection of chocolate biscuits to the table. He spoke as soon as he sat down.

"Leo Meyer worked closer, much closer to Scheffler than any of the other survivors; he was his servant. He even shaved him."

J J studied Yaakov Epstein closely and answered.

"He still hasn't made his mind up about testifying."

Yaakov looked pained. "He has to. This man they think is Scheffler is going to be convicted. When this happens, they will think they have caught the big fish, when all they've got is a tiddler. Scheffler, with all that blood of innocents on his hands, will be able to live the rest of his life without any fear."

"Do you chase Nazis all the time?"

"Twenty-four hours a day, every day. Now, drink your drinks and please take me to Leo Meyer."

J J shook her head, "We're going alone."

Rashid didn't understand. The man was genuine. They had been lucky so far but they couldn't go much further without adult help. "He wants to help us, J J."

"He's right," added Yaakov and then asked Rashid if he was leaving his Kit-Kat. Rashid nodded and Yaakov took and unwrapped the chocolate biscuit.

"He wants to catch war criminals, Rashid. I don't think he's bothered much about Michael."

Yaakov chewed fast and swallowed hard, "I want to help you get your friend as well. So far, you have been lucky and you've only come up against their lightweights…"

J J got up quickly from her seat. "We'll meet you back here at half-eleven." Rashid rose as well and smiled apologetically at the big man as they left the table.

* * * * *

Bob Brady rode two stops past Turner's Garage before getting off the bus. He walked back slowly and smoked three cigarettes. He had a lot to think about. Jake was on the telephone in Reception. He was cancelling appointments for the day. Packing cases littered the floor behind him.

"I want my son out of here right now!" Bob shouted

as soon as he was in the door.

Jake calmly finished his telephone conversation, "Sorry about that. Unforseen circumstances. Many thanks." He replaced the receiver and lifted the counter-flap for Bob to pass through. "Now then, Bob, I thought I explained yesterday. Michael won't get 'urt…"

"'E better bloody 'adn't, I'm tellin' you!"

"Did you pass on that message?"

"Yeh."

"Well, we just wait till eleven and things'll get sorted."

"I want 'im out now!"

Jake shook his head like a parent confronted by a silly, mischievous child. He reached out as if to give Bob a friendly, reassuring pat, but grabbed him roughly by the shoulder and pulled him through the packing cases to the swing doors at the back of reception. His manner had changed completely. Pushing Bob's face to the small square of glass in one of the doors, he told him to have a good look. No work was being done in the service area and there was no sign of the mechanics. A heavily built man wearing a dark suit was making some kind of inspection.

"If you think we're nasty, Bob, cuddle up to these lads. Razor blades for breakfast, 'im and 'is mates."

"I want to see Avril."

"She's out of it, Bob. Me too. The 'eavy Brigade's in charge. Look one of them in the face and it's the abattoir. The Movement doesn't like failure. And they get really angry with people who betray them. So don't do owt daft."

Bob swung his elbow, hitting Jake under the ribs. Jake's grip on him slackened and Bob wrenched himself free.

160

He pushed the door open and ran across the service area towards the back entry to the second loading bay. Several angry shouts followed him but he reached the door unchallenged. The Transit was still there, but parked deeper into the bay uncovering what Bob thought was an old inspection pit. The planks had been lifted revealing stairs that led to a large underground storeroom. Two other strangers were carrying a long, heavy, sealed crate from this storeroom and loading it on to a removal van. Bob ran between the vehicles and round the stairwell to the office where Michael was. Out of the corner of his eye, he saw a figure – grey, soft leather jacket – by the entrance, turn and raise an arm automatically. Bob looked towards him and recognised immediately the stubby Uzi sub-machine gun which was being aimed. Someone had brought one to the gun club a few months back. Weren't this lot his mates? He'd helped them. They couldn't use his son like this. I mean, some of them had to be fathers as well. They'd understand.

Posters of new cars for the nineteen-seventies blocked the view through the glass-panelled door into the office. Bob hesitated slightly – *razor blades for breakfast; Uzi submachine guns* – before pulling back the bolt that fastened the door on the outside. He pushed the door open violently.

Michael, hands and feet tied, was in a corner under a desk. Blood had caked thickly around a cut above his right eye. He turned his face to the wall when he saw who had come in. Bob pulled him out from under the desk as gently as he could and, with Michael still sitting on the floor, he knelt and tried to hug him. Michael twisted out of his arms.

161

"Don't touch me! They knew about t'photographs and where we took Leo, thanks to you."

"You've gorrit all wrong, lad. I'm not one of this lot. I just wanted a job. I've come to tek you 'ome."

Michael saw the other man before his father did and felt a strange quiver of satisfaction from knowing that he had never really trusted him. This was followed quickly by fear as he saw what the man was holding. Michael bit his lip and tensed himself. The first Bob Brady knew of the man's presence was the heavy, cold feel of metal pressed to his neck just below his ear. He recognised the voice immediately.

"A touching reunion," said Simon Leighton. "Nice to think, that after years of neglecting your son, you're now going to spend some time with him."

Bob made to get up from his kneeling position but Simon pushed the gun's barrel harshly into his neck. "Don't for one second imagine that I won't use this. I'd enjoy killing you, Brady. Getting rid of worthless items like you and our foreign guests is our speciality."

★ ★ ★ ★ ★

Leo held two small, broken pieces of bone, the remains of a moor animal's meal. He gestured a hammering action: "They made some people work... with big wooden mallets... breaking... pounding... pounding the bones... from the crematoria until they were dust. And they dumped what remained into the Vistula."

"You have to testify," said J J.

"But he can't," blurted Rashid, "if we want... want..."

Leo nodded and smiled with understanding. He was

ready to testify, he told them, but Michael's life was more important. J J and Rashid must go to the telephone at eleven o'clock and tell the fascists that Leo Meyer will give himself up to them in return for the boy's freedom.

On the telephone, J J wanted to argue, to make arrangements that would guarantee Michael's safety, but, not for the first time in this episode, she found she was not in control of what was happening. The call took less than a minute. The man spoke softly and sounded well-educated. There was something in the timbre that was familiar. He told J J she was being very sensible and that Meyer should be taken back to the farmhouse and left there alone. No one else should be anywhere near the farmhouse. They would know if anyone was. Once Meyer was in their hands, they would release Michael unharmed somewhere in the city. The only time a hint of anger showed in his voice was when J J asked him where that would be.

"No questions. Do as you're told and your friend will be all right. If you don't follow these instructions or if you involve the police, you'll find your friend in the river."

Chapter 18

They sat at a table by the window, behind the *E* in *CAFE*. J J pictured the word the correct way round and tried to remember which way the accent went in French – anything to distract herself from thoughts of Michael and Leo Meyer. Yaakov brought his cup down slowly from his lips.

"You have signed Leo Meyer's death warrant."

J J snapped back, "Leo decided himself."

"They won't let your friend go."

"They said they would."

Yaakov gave a sardonic laugh. "Michael knows too much. He stays away from home, sleeps rough. Such boys have accidents. The people who beat up Leo on the moor were local thugs, a unit known as Group 88 – H is the eighth letter of the alphabet; HH, *Heil Hitler*. Simple when you know, isn't it? I have reason to believe that a much more organised and ruthless group called The Harvesters is running things now."

"The Harvesters?"

"On November 3rd, 1943, most of the Jews in Majdanek, a camp in East Poland, and many in nearby workcamps, perhaps up to forty thousand, were put to death. Shot. Large numbers of SS and police were brought in for the purpose. This operation was code-named *Erntefest*, in English, the Harvest Festival."

Yaakov's explanation was delivered in the matter-of-fact manner of someone whose emotional responses has been dulled by familiarity with such statistics.

"You're just saying this to get us to give you Leo!"

"No, believe me, I'm not. I know how difficult this all

is for you, but I know these people. You *must* let me help you."

Up to that point in their second meeting with Yaakov, Rashid had been silent. He reached for J J's hand and squeezed it. "I think we should." He smiled at her, "I don't fancy a second bike-ride to Brereton Moor this morning."

Leo insisted on setting the fox free, "He's ready. Much longer and he'll not want to leave; he'll confuse captivity and freedom."

For a moment, the fox seemed reluctant to accept its liberty and sniffed the air and grass intently outside the dismantled pen. Leo shouted and stamped his foot and the fox shied away. Without a glance back at them, it trotted steadily up the slope through the wood with only a ghost of the wound showing in the movement of its right hind leg.

Yaakov was waiting at the roadside. He kept his promise not to try to dissuade Leo from what was planned, but did tell him that SS officer, Obersturmbannführer Scheffler was still active.

"He is inspiration to the neo-fascists who are growing in numbers all over Europe. The killer of thousands is breeding more killers! He has to be tried and punished."

Leo nodded but said nothing and started to shuffle across the road towards the farmhouse.

"You more than anyone else must know that these people are unlikely to let the boy go," Yaakov called after him.

"While there is a chance they will free him, we must take it," Leo answered without turning.

A bleary sun penetrated the mist which, like a deep, persistent headache, had covered the top of the moor all morning. J J remained silent, feeling the chill of defeat and worse, the nagging anxiety that there might have been another way to resolve the situation. Rashid saw what was happening and hugged her. "It's not over yet," he said.

J J looked at him and tried to raise a smile, "Not until the fat lady sings, eh?"

Rashid smiled back, but Yaakov told them that they had to get well clear of the moor right away.

"These people are thorough and dangerous. If they spot us anywhere near this place, your friend will be killed."

"As simple as that?" asked J J.

"Yes. You don't believe there are people who can act in this way?" Yaakov asked in return.

Struggling to keep herself from crying, J J nodded her head rapidly, "Oh, I do, yes, I do."

Simon Leighton was angry. The thrill of being on active service had not overcome awareness that his involvement was premature. But Avril and her tattooed thugs had bungled things and he had had to mobilise his unit of The Harvesters. If someone more competent had been in charge from the start, Meyer would be dead, Bauer would have been convicted in the belief that he was Scheffler, and the para-military wing could have gone on steadily and stealthily strengthening itself in support of the Deliverance Party's bid for electoral power. He glanced at his watch. They should be there by now.

It was two o'clock. The pilot brought the helicopter down delicately in the fine mist. At first, the sheep scattered in all directions like fragments from an explosion, but soon regathered and headed towards a quieter part of Brereton Moor's great expanse. Six men, all dressed as if they were going to take a long-distance hike, jumped out. The last turned and fastened down the polythene sheet that had been buffetted free during the flight, revealing the sign, GILMORE CONSTRUCTION, on the tail of the aircraft. Then he gave a thumbs-up sign and the pilot lifted the helicopter and skimmed across the Moor in the direction of Otley, scattering the sheep again.

The six men ranged in age from twenty-two to forty-five. Four had served with the British Army in the Falklands and Northern Ireland and two of those had also seen active service as mercenaries in Angola and Bosnia. The other two were products of The Harvesters' own military training. They separated, but all headed in the general direction of Hangman's Rocks. There, on the slope leading down to the road and below the mist that had hidden their advance, three took up covert positions from which they could watch the approaches to the farmhouse, while the others quartered the valley on both sides of the road in search of anyone who might frustrate their plans.

At precisely half-past three, sure that it was safe, the Harvesters radioed Simon Leighton and then moved to points closer to their target, blending with trees, bracken, stone walls, whatever cover was available. In place, they formed a protective ring about the farmhouse.

Once the all-clear was received at the garage, three

other members of the unit travelled in the Transit van to the farmhouse. It was a simple, smooth operation. There was no violence. They found Leo Meyer listening to the recordings of Hitler's speeches. He did not resist them.

★ ★ ★ ★ ★

Imran had watched Turner's all day. This was different, all this activity. Something odd was happening and it had nothing to do with garage work. The mechanics hadn't turned up except for the burly man who had called Imran *Geronimo*, but he didn't stay long. A group of smartly dressed men had taken over. They shut down the petrol pumps: *CLOSED UNTIL FURTHER NOTICE*; backed a removal van into the second loading bay, and removed *FOR SALE* signs from the cars on the forecourt.

Imran left the Mini and traversed the bottom of the terraced streets, Alma, Sebastapol, Inkerman and Balaclava, and stood at a bus stop near a small, corner-cafe. Two buses travelling along Herse Road stopped. The driver of the second shouted at him to stand somewhere else. Imran ignored him and watched, with increasing anxiety, the comings and goings at the garage. He heard another bus coming, the three thirty-three to Higley, and stepped back from the edge of the pavement. The bus slowed down but did not stop. When it had passed, he saw the removal van easing away from the bay entrance to allow the Transit to be driven out, off the garage forecourt and right in the general direction of Birch Lane and Brereton Moor. They were packing up. That's what they were doing. The fascists were leaving, getting away scot-free. Imran ran back to the Mini, not sure what he could do, but certain that he had to do something to stop them.

★ ★ ★ ★ ★

J J could not believe how complacent Yaakov was about what had happened; he seemed to have given up all together. She had ignored his warning about how ruthless and efficient The Harvesters were, and had suggested that they should try to follow them in the car after they picked up Leo. "We have to do something!" Yaakov acted as if he did not hear and drove slowly back to the cafe talking casually about chocolate from different countries: "American you can keep. I don't understand why they get excited about Hershey Bars… Now, Belgian chocolate; we're talking ecstasy now… In the Lebanon once, I had to survive for three days on one bar of cooking chocolate…" He kept telling them to take whatever they wanted from the box on the back seat. Twice he took bars for himself and, with the second, a leaky Picnic, nearly crashed the car into a hedge as he tried to shake the sticky wrapper from his sleeve.

J J was angry and felt let down by him, the big, ambling, useless clown. He'd probably overdosed on chocolate and damaged his brain. The cafe was packed with every table occupied except the one they had used that morning, the one by the window. June smiled and took the RESERVED sign away as Yaakov and the two young people sat down. J J refused, but Yaakov ordered cups of hot chocolate for her and Rashid.

"She makes it very rich." He looked at his watch and glanced out of the window. "You need a hot drink after

170

what has happened."

Even though his companions, caught up in thoughts about what might be happening to Michael and Leo, weren't listening, Yaakov chattered on, telling them about his life as a student in the U.S.A, as a conscript in the Israeli army and as an investigator for the International War Crimes Research Centre. Time passed slowly. Rashid studied the other people in the cafe, and wondered what they would say and do if he stood up and told them about Leo Meyer, about The Harvesters, about Michael. Would they believe him? Would they sympathise with an old Jew, with a half-caste boy? J J tried to think of other things: incomplete GCSE projects, the words to favourite songs, but her mind kept coming back to Michael and Leo. She pictured them in a concentration camp, sitting on bunk beds, Michael on top, both emaciated, both almost bald and wearing the faded, striped uniform, and both staring uncomprehendingly at the camera of her imagination. She resented Yaakov's jabbering about trivia. It was so uncaring, so coldly professional: this case was lost, so don't waste time, energy and words mourning those who had been sacrificed. He wasn't even looking at them as he talked; he was more interested in the street outside. Calm the kids down with a cup of chocolate and then be off. Who the hell did he think he was?

Another glance out of the cafe window told Yaakov it was time to go. He stood up suddenly. The Ford Transit had entered Herse Street and was heading towards Turner's Garage. He had guessed correctly. Yaakov looked at his watch: quarter to five. Traffic was heavy. They would probably use the rush hour, when the Ring Road and the access to the motorway became very busy, to transfer Leo to another vehicle and take him out of the area. There was a rumour that Scheffler wanted to kill Meyer himself. J J, still angry, stood up as well. Rashid told her to take it easy and placed a hand on her forearm. She shook it off.

"Off now, are you? Another case? People are just files and records to you, aren't they?"

Yaakov was still looking out of the window. He spoke calmly. "There might be something we can do. The garage across the way is the local headquarters for Group 88. My hope was that The Harvesters would come here. They have, and if we can confirm that your friend has been freed, we can try to help Leo Meyer."

Chapter 19

He knew it was close to hysteria, but Michael couldn't stop himself from giggling every time his captors referred to each other by a number: *THREE, put that box in the van; FOUR, see if FIVE and the others are`in position at the farmhouse.* He giggled most when ONE, Simon Leighton, did it. It just sounded so stupid.

ONE and TWO stood outside the office in the loading bay. ONE chose TWO to kill Michael, Leo Meyer and Bob Brady.

Simon Leighton was trying to brush a mark off the front of his trousers. It wouldn't budge and looked like oil. A three hundred pound suit: this was the kind of thing that happened when you had to step in at a moment's notice to clear up other people's messes. It made him very angry.

"One to get rid of. That was the original brief. Simple. One old man. Thanks to incompetence, we now have three."

"Three separate cars?"

"No, we'll do it here," he said, without raising his eyes from the stain. "This place is no good to us now. Burn it and the Transit. The bodies must be unrecognisable. The paint store. Should make a pretty blaze."

He was annoyed – he must have brushed up against a workbench – but tried not to let it show. "Oh, and TWO, the others can be left to the fire, but Meyer must be shot."

TWO, young, intense, unsmiling, had been at his sullen worst when Simon Leighton gave him the order. He resented being made to work like a donkey all day shifting crates on to a van; that wasn't what he had been trained to do. He smiled briefly when Leighton told him to execute the prisoners. This was more like it.

They moved from the loading bay and through the service area at a snail's pace. The Bradys still had their hands tied behind their backs and their feet hobbled. Meyer wasn't tied at all, but was the slowest. He looked so bad that TWO thought he would be doing the Jew a favour by killing him; put him out of his agony, as you would a suffering animal. He was so slow. TWO curbed his impatience and, for a moment, he was back nursing a screaming comrade in a dew-heavy hedgerow in Armagh. Impatience led to indiscipline, rash judgements and ill-timed action.

The Jew stopped and leant heavily against the workbench. He was breathing hard. He spoke to no one in particular. "You know, in Auschwitz, I did nothing…"

TWO prodded him with his gun. "No speeches. Move!"

Leo flapped his hands as if he couldn't care less what happened to him. He was going to be killed so it might as well be there as in some other part of the building or in a lonely Pennine lane. "I was just a boy but I could have…"

"Move!"

Leo put a hand behind him on the workbench to steady himself. He stroked the deeply scarred wooden surface firmly, rhythmically as if preparing himself mentally to take his last few steps to death. *I am not Musselman… I am not Musselman…* The workbench was littered with metal shavings. They pierced his fingers as he edged them behind a large vice.

"I *should* have fought them."

"I don't mind killing you here."

Leo eased himself away from the bench as if to go on, but his hand lingered on the work surface. Michael saw what he was doing and almost whimpered out loud with the thought of what the thug would do.

"Now, I am a weak old man…"

TWO was at the end of his tether. "Shut up and move, you stupid Jew!"

TWO turned slightly from Leo and gestured for Michael and his father to move on. Leo continued to talk while his hand grasped a huge spanner and swung it – Michael looked back; it seemed to arc so slowly up from the bench, oddly cold and ugly in Leo's thin fingers – hard onto the side of TWO's head. His ear burst, and blood flowed heavily. For a moment, it seemed as if he wasn't going to fall. His lips twitched in a smile, a brief, defiant attempt to deny what was happening, and claim he was still in control, before he fell heavily to the floor. The gun went off as he went down, the bullet ricocheting harmlessly down the far end of the service area.

Leo hadn't the strength to halt his swinging arm and toppled to the floor. From there, he shouted, "Run, Michael, run!"

Pressing on the workbench with his tied hands, in an awkward, half-shuffling, half-vaulting motion, Bob Brady stumbled to the end of the long stroke of the L-shape that was the service area. Michael didn't move.

Leo tried to give his voice some authority. "Stupid! Go! Leave me!" but it sounded thin, reedy. He was so tired. The boy was saying something. Leo couldn't hear him properly. There was a surging in his ears. Sound came to him as if he was underwater.

"… not… leaving you…"

Michael knelt, twisted himself round, gripped Leo as best he could and then tried to stand pulling the old man with him. Leo couldn't or wouldn't help. He felt like lead. Michael screamed at his father to come back and help him. TWO was beginning to come round. Bob Brady staggered from the workbench past the old yellow Escorts to a door and banged ineffectually at it.

"They've tekken t'bloody key!"

★ ★ ★ ★ ★

A soft cough from Rashid in the back seat. J J spoke.

"Are we just going to sit here?"

They had watched several men leave the garage separately and drive off in the forecourt cars that had originally been for sale. Yaakov assured his young friends that Leo Meyer could not be in those vehicles. "Michael could be," J J retorted.

The car radio was on at low volume; the second movement from Beethoven's Pastoral Symphony, that Rashid's class had discussed in a music lesson. Rashid had startled the long-suffering music teacher, Mr Hilditch, by saying that it reminded him of a stream. It was odd, considering Rashid's feelings about the countryside and about classical music. *Excellent, Rashid, excellent.*

Yaakov stopped moving his head gently to the rhythm. "All we can do is wait, observe, hope we get an opportunity to do something."

"We've got to get closer."

"You still don't understand, do you? You are not in some Disney film. These people are real and they are

176

killers."

"Have you got a gun?"

Yaakov turned and looked hard at her as if he was considering whether or not he should answer the question. "Yes," he said, and looked down to the garage once again. "It's at the bottom of the box."

Rashid rummaged carefully among the bars of chocolate until he felt an odd, bulkier shape. It wasn't metal. It was a heavy plastic replica of a Colt 45, sticky with chocolate and toffee. Rashid pulled it out. In the driver's mirror, Yaakov saw Rashid's puzzled face. "It shoots small, jelly-bean type sweets," he told them. "I picked it up in Ohio or somewhere. I think I'm out of ammunition. Sorry."

J J couldn't wait any longer. "I'm going down there." She got out of the car before Yaakov could grab her. Moving more quickly than she thought him capable of, Yaakov got out on the driver's side.

"You won't help your friend or Leo! And you could be hurt, perhaps killed."

J J ignored him. She knew all that. She also knew that she was no good at the game of chess, of trying to anticipate what her opponent would/could do if she moved one of her pieces in a certain direction. Her father, a keen chess player, had tried twice to teach her when she was eleven and on both occasions, J J had tipped the board scattering the pieces. She was fed up of going over and over in her mind what might happen if… and concluding that caution was the best policy. She started to cross the road to the garage with the intention of tipping the chess board on to the floor.

Rashid got out of the back seat of the Sierra, shrugged

his shoulders at Yaakov and followed J J. Before Yaakov left the car to catch up with them, he reached back into the car for a bar of chocolate. As he did so, he heard a sound, in the midst of the traffic, that he thought he recognised from those terrifying days in the Lebanon, a sound that was nothing like the tarted up gunshots of the films. Yaakov left the chocolate and picked up his trusty, plastic Colt 45.

Simon Leighton looked out from Avril's office, across the forecourt. The streets were busy, very busy. There were a lot of people, especially Asians, on foot. A factory must be emptying nearby. Traffic was heavy and slow. The timing was perfect. He had dismissed the group that brought Meyer back from the farmhouse. They had changed back into casual clothes and driven off, joining the thick stream of traffic coming down Herse Road and heading for the motorway. Only four of the unit plus himself were left. TWO was attending to the guests and the others were waiting in the removal van. He would go with them as far as the first motorway services where he had left his car that morning. Worcester, Bristol, Newark, Newcastle, Glasgow; Enfield, Carlisle, Hull, Peterborough and Chester: each member of his unit of The Harvesters would be back home by half-nine/ten enjoying a drink at the local, or a video with the family, and feeling the satisfaction of having done a good job. He could probably pop back into the hospital to polish up a presentation he had to give on extending the provision of private beds at Brancaster General and its satellite hospitals.

He stretched contentedly, his arms out above his head, his back arched. His muscular body, he thought, was like a strong yew bow ready to fire an arrow into the monster of multi-ethnicity that was dragging Britain into its swamp. The metaphor was a bit overdone, but was one worth coming back to: metaphor, symbol were powerful weapons in the struggle.

His body slumped back into the seat when he heard it. It was too early and too noisy. TWO had to go to the paint store, tie their legs tightly once more, execute Meyer and then set the timer of the incendiary device. TWO would use the silencer. TWO could be impatient, but when given a specific task, was thorough, a soldier who would stick to the pattern right down to the last, minute detail. Something had gone wrong.

When Simon Leighton entered the service area, he was reassured to see that, although Meyer, Brady and the boy were not in sight, TWO was on his feet and, most important of all, was clutching his weapon. Leighton took out his gun, a Desert Eagle pistol. It would not have been his first choice, but he thought how ironically fitting it was that Meyer would be executed by a weapon manufactured in Israel. He ordered TWO to set the incendiary device in the paint store and tell the others to get the van out of the bay and ready to move: "I'll see to the Jew."

J J and Rashid were twenty-five metres away, Yaakov another thirty, when the wide overhead door to the loading bay started to rise. They stopped. Steadily, the door lifted to reveal a fresh-faced young man in a grey leather jacket pulling on the chain-hoist and three others squeezed into the cabin of a removal van. One was pressing a bloody cloth to the side of his head. The engine was running. The young man nodded casually and smiled at the approaching group and then looked questioningly at his friends. As the driver started to move the van slowly out of the bay, J J ran forward and sat in its path. Rashid joined her.

"Where's Michael? Where's our friend?" she shouted above the noise of the traffic. "And where's Leo Meyer?"

Yaakov broke into a run and as he did so, put a fist to his mouth and pretended he was biting on a comforting bar of chocolate. This encounter could be very nasty.

Still in first gear, the driver kept easing the van forward. The young man walked alongside, opened the passenger door but did not climb in. Half of him was hidden by the door.

"No idea what you're talking about, love, but I'd move if I was you," he shouted back at J J.

It was instinct and the certain knowledge that The Harvesters – even this soft-featured young man – were trained killers, that made Yaakov forget about chocolate bars and pull his jelly-bean Colt from his inside pocket. He raced, placed himself between the young people and the van and, in a crouching position, took aim. He was right. From there, and only ten metres away, he could see under the van door and confirm that the young man in the leather jacket was now carrying a gun. It was pressed against his leg, pointing downwards; probably an Uzi.

"If he brings it up, I'm finished," thought Yaakov, "and so are these young ones."

The van stopped. The gun was drawn upwards and out of sight. Yaakov shouted: "Don't! I *will* fire!" The young man said something to the others and then stepped clear of the van door. He had got rid of the gun.

"It worked!" said Yaakov quietly, "They've fallen for it." But the thugs weren't looking at him or his gun; their eyes were focusing beyond him on the silent crowd of people that had formed on the garage forecourt and that was quickly shaping itself into a formidable wall about the whole garage. Yaakov looked puzzled. J J, who was on her feet and had turned to see what was happening, shouted that the cavalry had arrived. Rashid corrected her.

"Wrong, it's the Indians."

The information Imran carried back to Birch Lane had spread quickly around the restaurants, youth clubs, grocers, street corners, back yards, kitchens of the area. It was as if the word he brought back was what the Asian community had been waiting to hear, a call to action, action which would be a release valve for all the humiliation, hurt, fear and frustration they felt as the bombings and beatings had steadily increased. No one questioned what Imran was saying. Several added their own stories and suspicions about Turner's Garage: how they had been refused service; how they had seen lights on at strange hours; how they had always felt there was something evil about the place.

Asian young people, holidaying school children and the unemployed, were the first to gather. Imran cautioned them: the racists had to be stopped, but there was to be no violence unless they started it. Older members of the community joined them, men and women. Shops, restaurants and businesses closed early; in the homes, gas jets under bubbling pans were turned off. Tahir had watched from his office window. He was curious, but did not go into the street to find out what was happening: odd things were taking place in Hong Kong and he had

181

to keep an eye on his personal Far East Investment portfolio.

Yaakov looked behind him. People, black and white, men, women and children, were still shoaling down the terraced streets, and across Herse Road to join the thickening ring about the garage. Traffic had been forced to come to a halt, and drivers were standing by their cars to see what was going on. Several police cars were bleating their way apologetically down Birch Lane.

Chapter 20

Simon Leighton strode purposefully towards the captives. They were in the bottom section of the service area, the stubby part of the L. He knew this from the noise they were making in their futile attempt to escape. Striding purposefully: yes, he thought, that was what he was doing in life with the Movement: striding purposefully forward in the creation of a new Britain. His stride lengthened even more. His whole body was sharply alert and straining to bring this mission to a successful conclusion. He pictured himself crossing the workshop, his distinct, even facial features, and his muscular, erect body, a perfect specimen of a racial elite, were it not for that missing inch. Simon Leighton slowed down and shortened his stride. Ever since he had achieved physical maturity, he had suffered because of that missing inch. He wanted to be six foot. He told everyone he was six foot. He was five foot eleven.

When Simon Leighton found them behind the Escorts, the boy had managed to climb on to a bench and was kicking out panes of glass in a window. The Jew was trying to untie the knots binding Brady's hands. He herded them to the paint store. Enough time had been wasted. The old man fell a couple of times; they had no stamina and also gave in easily; racial, genetic weaknesses. He checked that TWO's work was done. It was. The incendiary device was at the foot of the shelves and around it TWO had piled aerosol cans and overalls soaked in paint-cleaning fluid.

The sad procession shuffled to a halt in the far corner where Leighton pointed. He fitted a silencer, lifted the gun at arm's length and held it to the old man's temple. It was all so exhilarating to feel the power the Movement had given him. He was about to end a life, a worthless life. Jews and other foreign elements plagued Europe. Fifty years before, one man had had the courage to proclaim this. If they didn't leave voluntarily, there was *no solution other than extermination*. He breathed in deeply and felt slightly dizzy. Regardless of what the other Harvesters believed, this would be the first time Simon Leighton had killed. He had imagined it many times before, always as a clean, quick, humane operation; a simple, workmanlike function of being a soldier. Is that how it really is? He pressed the gun harder against the victim's head but did not pull the trigger. He felt his arm tiring. Hesitation? Doubt? This was foolish, weak. Leighton quoted to himself the words The Harvesters had taken as their motto, words spoken by Himmler to his SS Obergruppenführers: *Our concern, our duty, is our people and our blood*. The gun barrel slipped from the soft, vulnerable depression of Meyer's temple to his cheekbone, his high, hard and arrogant Jewish cheekbone and Leighton felt the truth of his cause flooding his conscience once more. People like this contaminated the earth!

Leo Meyer turned to face his murderer. "Michael," he said quietly, "I forgot to tell you. The fox is free now." Leighton squeezed the trigger.

The gun did not fire. Leighton couldn't believe it. He pulled the pistol to him and quickly checked the mechanism. The safety catch was still on. TWO had made the first mistake and he had made a second by not checking earlier, a lapse in the habitual thoroughness he took pride in. It was easily remedied.

As Michael Brady had grown, so had his ability to find comfort in bleak circumstances. For one scrap of a moment, he saw the paint store as a childhood den, small, enclosed, with no natural light; a place where he would have enjoyed playing on rainy days. As Leighton raised his gun for the second time, Michael looked down at the floor. His love for Leo Meyer would not let him watch such a desecration of the old man's body.

Not a shot, but a long, gutteral scream ripped the quiet of the paint store. Michael saw his father blunder forward in an effort to shoulder charge Leighton. Bound as he was, it could only be a clumsy, off-balance effort to slow the killer down. Michael saw this and quickly slid to the ground extending his whole body across the floor. Leighton staggered backwards into Michael's legs and crashed to the floor with Bob Brady half on top of him smothering the gun. As they went down, Leighton's finger tightened on the trigger once again.

When Michael pulled himself upwards into a sitting position, he heard his name being called from somewhere outside the paint store, and he saw a badly winded Simon Leighton trying to pull himself out from under a very still Bob Brady. A band of blood, like an arm being slowly raised in a stiff-arm salute, was seeping steadily from his father's right shoulder. It trickled alongside the gun which had broken free from Leighton's grasp.

Seconds later, J J, Rashid, Yaakov and Imran found them. Michael had shuffled on his bottom to where he could kick Simon Leighton repeatedly in the ribs and Leo Meyer was sitting on his face.

Yaakov retrieved Leighton's gun and, while J J and Rashid saw to their friend, helped Leo to his feet. Bob

Brady moaned and rolled away from Leighton. Yaakov heard more footsteps in the workshop. The police. He hadn't much time. He took out the gun and lowered it to within a foot of Leighton's head. Leighton screamed. J J shouted and Rashid moved to stop him. Yaakov pulled the trigger. A strawberry cheesecake flavoured jelly bean spat out of the barrel and smacked a terrified Simon Leighton between the eyes.

When they discovered the crates of weapons on the removal van at Turner's Garage, the local police sealed the premises, put them under guard, and called in a special anti-terrorist unit from London. At eleven-thirty in the evening, before that unit had arrived, the incendiary device ignited TWO's little bonfire in the paint store and Turner's Garage was quickly ablaze. The removal van was driven clear. A crowd gathered and cheered. The fire officers stopped the fire from spreading elsewhere but did nothing to save the building.

At about the same time in Brancaster General Hospital, an exhausted Michael stood with his mother by Bob Brady's bed. He told her he would stay, just as he had done with Leo, but his mother shook her head. She was going to do that.

In the corridor just outside the room, J J, Rashid and Imran waited for their friend.

★ ★ ★ ★ ★

"A temporary setback, nothing more."

Scheffler did not reply to Gilmore. He had not slept and his body ached all over. This business should have been over and done with; should have been finished by himself fifty years before. A nick, a speck of blood on his chin would have been enough, or a damning patch of dullness on the instep of his boots – those would have been adequate reasons for executing Leo Meyer. But the boy had been careful, very careful.

Other titles in the
Spindlewood Paperback series

No Roof in Bosnia
Els de Groen
Translated by Patricia Crampton

Five teenagers – three boys and two girls – hide out
on a mountain in Bosnia whilst the war
swirls around them.

*Like no other book it captures the futility and heartache of
ethnic intolerance… a powerful and realistic story to challenge
and extend children's thinking.
(Anne Faundez in Junior Education)*

*This novel is a truly compelling story of human courage and
frailty in which there are no easy answers to be found.
(Books for Keeps)*

*In the reading of this tale we come to understand the pain and
the human consequences of not-so-distant politics… The
teenagers are sharply characterised, and the tensions – sexual
as well as ethnic – are allowed to emerge…
(Philip Pullman in The Guardian)*

The novel was short-listed for the Marsh Award in 1998
and was the IBBY Honours UK novel in translation.

ISBN : 0-907349-22-6

The Snow Globe
Anne Merrick

The Snow Globe is Anne Merrick's third novel for
Spindlewood and a paperback original.

It is a sensitive and fast-paced story telling the
experiences of Bella, a young girl whose mother goes
mysteriously missing. In Bella's attempts to find her she
is helped by the streetwise Matty. Matty's snow globe
holds a story within itself which seems to reflect
Bella and Matty's plight. A strange story which
Matty sees as his destiny.

Many readers will remember Anne Merrick's very
successful novel *Someone came knocking* – a title
commended for the Carnegie and also selected as
the IBBY UK Honours novel for 1995.

ISBN : 0-907349-24-2